Future Tense

Future Tense
Created By: V.B. Kennedy

Written By: V.B. Kennedy
www.vbkennedy.com

Published by Inkpendent Publishing

Printed in the United States of America

1st Edition / Printed: June 2019

Inkpendent Publishing
ISBN-13: 978-0615834498
ISBN-10: 0615834493

Edited By: Robert Kennedy
www.rkedits.com

Illustrated By: Terry Huddleston
thuddleston.deviantart.com

For my parents, who gave me a memorable past
and a promising future.

-V.B. Kennedy

The trouble with our times is that the future is not what it used to be. - Paul Valéry

Prologue

The scribe held his creation up to the light, admiring his skill in its craftsmanship. He twisted and turned it, transfixed by the light glinting off its gilded clip. His eyes traced the length of the tubular shape, its red hue a reflection of the passion he had put into his construct. He thought the herringbone design was a classic touch considering it was a last minute addition. The illusion of black stitching running across the ruby cylinder created a novelty effect. He removed the cap and brushed the nib against his finger, releasing a small black blot of what looked like ink. He rubbed his fingers together changing the stain into a smudge and then watched it disappear from his skin. He smiled, content with his successful endeavor. He knew his invention would change destinies. It was meant to whether they knew it or not.

"It's time," he commented to himself.

1
Once Upon a Time

The sounds of sickly sweet pop songs and thumping bass of trance tunes blaring from mammoth speakers near the spinning amusement rides, wafted through the cool Sunday night. Under the colorful blaze of blinking lights, the small herd of teenagers wandered from one game booth to another, attempting to win prizes that were worth a fraction of what they gambled. They continued along, besieged by several carnival barkers trying to entice them with their cheap, fuzzy trophies. The smell of popcorn and cotton candy surrounded them, threatening temptation to get seconds or thirds, although their stomachs were beginning to ache from feeding off of the junk food. It was the last night for the county fair and faux freedom, with school starting up again the next day. The winter air felt brisk as opposed to the Arctic blast that sometimes invaded their short breaks, which usually forced them to bundle up like Eskimos. Instead, they were all dressed in light jackets, silently appreciating Florida's erratic weather.

Mike Gutierrez, whose dark locks danced with the cold, breezing air, led the group to the milk bottle booth and exchanged his last five dollars for three baseballs. The tattooed carnie, who was missing more teeth than a seven-year-old, smiled unapologetically at Amber Daniels, the prettiest female of the group. She attempted to ignore the creepy stranger as she watched Mike knock down all the milk bottles on his first try. The group cheered enthusiastically as if he had medaled in an Olympic sport. The carnie begrudgingly gave Mike a giant pink, stuffed bear, which he quickly handed to Amber who cuddled it as if it were her first born. They slowly walked away from the booth as the dark cloud of the inevitable began to stalk them once more.

"I can't believe we go back to school tomorrow," said Mike. He winced as he realized that his lament signaled a whine greater than he had intended.

Heath Wells had a little more on his mind than his friend. As much as he dreaded the next day, Washington Irving High's former quarterback had something to look forward to.

"I don't know how I'm going to wake up in the morning," he said glumly, thinking how he had gotten used to staying up until three in the morning and sleeping in until one or two in the afternoon. He was positive it would take him at least a week to reset his circadian rhythm. "But at least I get my car back tomorrow," he added more cheerfully. As Heath said this, he realized his dilemma. How could he pick up his car when he didn't have one? "Who wants to give me a lift?" he asked, already knowing which one of his friends would lunge at the alluring bait he had presented.

"I can do it," Mike volunteered. "We can go right after school."

"Thanks," replied Heath, knowing that Mike would willingly be water boarded if Heath should ever ask.

As they continued to walk, Amber squealed with excitement as she saw a tall, red canvas tent and an advertisement with exotic lettering, for a fortune teller named Madam Souska.

Amber, who had had a crush on Heath since his

first winning football game, grabbed him by the arm like an arcade crane that had found a prize and began to drag him towards the tent pleading, "Come with me. I want know if they're going to make me captain of the cheerleading squad." She was grateful the weather wasn't too cold for her to wear her denim mini-skirt, in hopes Heath would spend the night checking out her long, tan legs but the only time he looked at them was to point out that one of her shoe laces had come undone.

Heath groaned internally and rolled his eyes as she dragged him and the pink bear away from their amused friends towards the obscured opening. Amber's dirty-blonde ponytail swayed as she moved. As attractive as he found her, he wasn't interested in being alone with her much less finding out about her so-called "future".

Heath and Amber walked through the flaps of the tent, pushing through a thick curtain of colorful beads that sounded like they were tsk-tsking the couple for being gullible, as the plastic globules fell back into place. Amber couldn't help but feel like they had just been swallowed alive and would spend their eternity with the lone figure sitting at the small round table in the center of the barren room. The fortune teller gestured to an ancient wooden chair across from where she sat. Amber's enthusiasm to hear her future seemed to have been left behind with their friends as she tried to block out the frightening middle-aged woman with her pink prize.

"Why don't you go first," Amber mumbled from behind the fuzzy trophy in her arms, whose permanent smile seemed to be mocking her fears. Amber quickly removed pink stray hairs from her tongue.

Unafraid, Heath sighed deeply and sat in the rickety empty chair and was surprised when it didn't instantly collapse under his weight. The heavy scent of patchouli began to burn in his nose. Unlike Amber, the only thing he felt was boredom. He placed a twenty-dollar bill on the table and laid his hand out, palm up, like a dead fish. Heath was startled and jumped in his seat when the silent fortuneteller loudly exclaimed "No!"

Somehow, Amber's fears became contagious as Heath timidly asked, "Tarot cards?"

"I don't like to use tarot cards," replied the fortuneteller, "I'm going to need one of your shoes instead."

Heath stared dumbfound at the woman, surprised that she asked for a shoe and because he didn't find her that unattractive. He couldn't tell if her large eyes were blue or green, but they were mesmerizing. Her dark, wavy mane, framed an oval face with a small upturned nose and pouty lips.

Perhaps if she shaved her chin and removed the three warts on her face, he thought. *Make it four warts,* as he did a quick mental recount.

"A shoe?" Heath repeated incredulously.

The fortuneteller's whiskey stained sigh almost knocked Heath off his seat. "I can't tell you where you're going until I know where you've been."

Heath looked over at Amber hoping she could make sense of the fortuneteller's request but she looked just as confused as he did. As Heath leaned over and began to untie his right shoe, he realized that the fortuneteller didn't have one of those strange accents one would hear in a vampire movie. She sounded…local. He quickly regarded her more carefully as he sat up and noticed that even her purple paisley skirt and white blouse seemed quite mundane.

How odd, he mused.

The fortuneteller winced as Heath handed his shoe over to her. The smell could kill a small animal. *Or even a skinny, future seeing woman*, she thought without amusement.

"I need another gimmick," she said under her breath and regretted it immediately. She realized she should have held her breath and aired out the shoe as long as possible. When she felt the foul shoe was less hazardous, she put her hands around it and closed her eyes. Unlike most people who can only see darkness when their eyes are closed, visions immediately began to appear for her eyes only. An image of an unconscious Heath sprawled on the street next to a totaled motorcycle filled her head.

"Hmm," she said with sincerity. This customer was a little more fascinating than she thought. "Interesting. A motorcycle accident. Shame about your arm."

Heath and Amber both stared at the stranger with a mix of awe and shock.

How could she know that? Heath thought to himself.

But before he could pursue that thought further, the fortuneteller continued. "I'm beginning to see dates," she said quietly.

"Anyone cute?" Heath joked, desperately trying

to ease his rattled nerves. Amber quickly slapped Heath in the back of his head which amused him more than his lame joke, as he chuckled to himself.

"Dates that have not yet happened and days that will never be…that's strange."

"What?" Heath asked, concern in his voice.

The fortuneteller opened her eyes and looked directly at Heath. "You disappear," she said matter of fact.

"I die?" Heath asked, trying not to sound too panicked.

"No. You disappear. I can't see you anymore," she said with a hint of worry. This feeling she emoted was more for herself than it was for Heath. Madam Souska, better known as Laura Stein to the I.R.S., always worried that her abilities would one day vanish and it seemed that day had finally come.

Not today. Not yet, she thought to herself. *But how does someone disappear from the future?* She had one more trick up her sleeve. In her pocket, actually. She pulled out a stack of tarot cards which she kept on her in case she ever had difficulty reading a person. They were a last resort should seeing through a nebulous future hinder her abilities. It was the third time she ever needed those cards. Heath eyed the tarot cards suspiciously.

"I thought you don't use tarot cards."

"I said I don't like to use them," she corrected. "I usually don't need to" *I almost never need to* she thought to herself but she felt that fact would cause her customer to flee and that was the last thing she wanted. Her curiosity was truly piqued. She had to know why some snot-nosed nobody was messing with her mojo. The fortune teller handed the cards to Heath and instructed him, "You need to shuffle these and ask yourself: Where am I going?"

Heath felt slightly foolish as he closed his eyes and began to shuffle. "Where am I going?" he said unenthusiastically.

The fortuneteller stopped him after a moment and took the cards back. She then placed three cards from the deck, face down on the table. She flipped over one of the cards, revealing an image Heath did not understand. "The fool," she said pointing to the card. "That's you." Under her breath she quickly added, "Fitting." She flipped over the next card whose skeletal image Heath recognized before she even announced it. "The Death card," she said.

"I thought you said I don't die!" Heath exclaimed. The fortuneteller nearly laughed in Heath's face for two reasons. She was relieved to discover there was nothing wrong with her clairvoyance and also because she found his ignorance amusing. But again, she was determined to complete his reading to satisfy her own curiosity and knew that humiliating him would not turn out well.

"No, no, no," she reassured. "The card you want to avoid is the Tower card. The Death card just means your life is going to go through some major changes." When she saw that Heath relaxed slightly in his seat, she flipped over the third and last card. "Uh-oh," she said when she saw the image of a burning steeple.

"What?" he asked, clearly shaken.

The fortuneteller leaned back as far as possible in her chair as if lightning would strike Heath at any moment and said, "I can't tell you exactly how or why but your life is about to take a serious turn for the worse. There will be a huge upheaval that will affect you and even those around you, forever. Something catastrophic is coming and only you may be able to prevent it." Satisfied that her abilities were intact and she was able to read Heath as easily as a billboard, the fortuneteller turned her attention to Amber and smiled as she asked cheerily, "Are you ready for your reading now?"

Heath and Amber walked out of the fortuneteller's tent, both quiet as the dead. Amber frowned with annoyance while Heath was lost in thought.

"What the hell was that?" Amber spat out as she loosened her ponytail. She was upset that she would actually have to wait until next year to find out if she made captain of the cheerleading squad. She angrily pushed her dirty blond hair behind her ears and crinkled her freckled nose in disgust. Though she was still young, Amber was running out of virtues and patience was nowhere on her limited list.

"I don't know," Heath answered, still confused by the night's strange events.

"Do you believe her?" asked Amber incredulously.

"I don't know," Heath repeated. "She knew about my motorcycle accident."

Unconvinced, Amber said, "That was in the local news. She probably read it in the Sentinel or saw it on T.V." But Heath was truly spooked by the fortuneteller's words.

"It was still pretty creepy. Something's going to affect me and those around me. Something catastrophic." He could still hear her words as if she were repeating them in his ears.

"It's probably just a pop quiz," Amber told him, hoping she could talk some sense into him. As cute as he was, this was becoming a real turn off.

"Maybe," he said absentmindedly.

"So much for tonight," Amber mumbled disappointedly as she took out her cell phone and dialed a number. She had been hoping to seduce Heath later that night but she really wasn't up for making out with a whiner. "Hey, where are you guys?" Amber said into her phone desperately when she heard Mike's voice on the line. She wanted to rejoin her friends as soon as possible to recover some semblance of normalcy in her life and hope they could convince Heath not to be such an idiot.

After a few seconds, Amber replied to the voice on the phone, "We'll meet you there." Amber ended the call and led a distracted Heath toward their friends and what she hoped would be a better evening.

Heath dropped his key ring into the glass dish on the accent table in the foyer, and heard it land with a *clink*. He stared at his house key for a brief moment thinking how lonely it looked without his car key next to it and looked forward to reuniting them again soon.

Even though the fair was going to be open until ten o'clock that night, Heath had made up an excuse to leave before nine and found someone to drop him off at his house. He had lied about having a stomachache, but he felt as if it had become a self-fulfilling prophecy as a dull pain was slowly building up, deep inside his gut.

As he walked down the hallway to his room, he could hear the sound of his parent's television. He stood outside their door, tempted to go inside and talk to them but then changed his mind. It wasn't that he thought they would dismiss his fears. It was just that lately, he had been feeling as if he had let them down as a son. Although they had never spoken of it, he felt that losing his ability to play football had destroyed them as much as him. He was on the verge of failing his senior year and now he was considering storming their room to tell them about the crazy lady who had predicted his doom. They had been his biggest cheerleaders, yet he had given them nothing to cheer about. He walked away and continued to his room.

Heath yawned deeply. He had gotten up early that morning to help his dad mow the lawn and after tonight's misadventure, he was now physically and emotionally exhausted. He went to the bathroom to relieve himself and brush his teeth. He returned to his room, took off his shirt and lay down in his bed, not even bothering to remove the covers. And as much as he dreaded it, Heath went to sleep.

Like so many times since his accident, Heath woke with a start, panting heavily as he sat up in bed. He groaned when he glanced at his alarm clock and saw it was almost three in the morning. He wiped sweat from his brow as he recalled the nightmare his consciousness had just saved him from. He had been dreaming about his accident again but unlike the expected rerun, Madam

Souska made a special guest appearance as one of the rescue workers who came to his aid that night. He vaguely remembered that in his dream, the fortune teller, dressed in a dark blue EMT uniform, kneeled at his side and held his hand in hers, searching for a pulse from his unresponsive body. She shook her head grimly and told her partner who stood on the other side of Heath's lifeless form that he was gone.

She then stood up and said matter of fact, "Just as well. Everyone would have died if he had lived."

Heath threw himself back, his head landing on his pillow with a soft thud. He rubbed his eyes hoping he could wipe away the night terror he felt but the anxiety continued to linger like a bad memory. He closed his eyes and waited. It would be two hours before sleep invited him back to dreamland.

2
A Stitch in Time

On Monday morning, Heath sat in his Social Studies class, wondering how time had compressed two weeks into what felt like only two days. He yawned deeply as he watched his teacher, Mrs. Stevens, stand in front of the class clutching a small stack of papers. She was a former model who never failed coming to school wearing tight shirts that accentuated her curvy figure. Today's top was emerald green with a low V-neck, which the boys looked forward to seeing every three weeks or so. She stood by her dingy steel gray desk which was littered with graded papers that never seemed to get filed and framed pictures of her three young kids. Though she must have been in her mid-forties, most of the girls thought she wore more make-up than she needed. As usual, most of the boys were staring at her but she had Heath's attention for a different reason. Her mouth was smiling but her eyes said something else. Something sinister.

"Good morning class," she began. "As happy as I am to see you all again, I'm curious as to how many dead brain cells the Grim Reaper claimed during your winter vacation so I would like to start the new year with a pop quiz."

Though the class groaned in unison, Heath relaxed in his seat, recalling Amber's words of wisdom from the night before.

"A pop quiz," he said to himself relieved, but then quickly came to his senses. "Oh, no! A pop quiz!"

Mrs. Stevens systematically handed a few sheets of paper to the first student in each row, who proceeded to pass on the bad news to the students sitting behind them. Most of the teens whimpered when they received their quiz, as if they had already been given failure notices. Heath could swear some of the students' eyes glimmered with tears. He felt misty-eyed as well, as he wrote his name on his paper. He was already failing her class and wondered how many more "Fs" it would take before his grade point average dropped into the negatives.

Noting the sea of slack jawed students staring down at their papers with disbelief, Mrs. Stevens clapped her hands two times and said, "C'mon guys. These quizzes aren't going to fail themselves."

Heath rolled his eyes and proceeded to write the date but immediately realized he had written the wrong year.

"It's a new year, Heath," he muttered as he scratched out the wrong year and corrected it. So far, the only answer he knew was his name.

I'm pathetic, he thought to himself.

There was a knock on the classroom door and a student walked in holding a small white slip of paper in her hand that would grant a student permission to leave class. The students looked at the office aide with anticipation, as if she was about to declare one of them the winner of the Publishers Clearing House Sweepstake. The office aide handed the paper to Mrs. Stevens who glossed over it quickly.

She looked up at Heath and said, "Heath. Your counselor would like to see you. You can go as soon as you're done with your quiz."

Rolling his eyes, Heath flipped over his blank quiz and announced, "I'm done." He grabbed his book bag and headed for the classroom exit. In his hurry to meet with his executioner, Heath didn't realize he had dropped his pen.

Mr. Amara looked thoughtfully at Heath who sat in a chair across from him. Heath couldn't help but feel as if it were déjà vu.

I wonder what HE sees in my future, thought Heath.

Though he was the oldest of several school counselors, Mr. Amara was the most popular. He was a good listener even when a student was spewing an obscenity-laced tirade about a teacher. He was also fairly successful in talking sense into his students. Heath usually counted himself as one of Mr. Amara's fans but today he was angry with the messenger because he didn't want to hear the message.

The counselor furrowed his graying brows, creating deeper crevasses in his already wrinkled forehead.

"Do you know why you're here?" asked Mr. Amara.

Heath averted his eyes from the counselor's face. There were times when he found Mr. Amara's gaze a bit too intense, as if he were trying to read him.

"I do, but I would like to see if you know too," answered Heath, getting lost in the blue and green swirly pattern of the counselor's tie.

Mr. Amara was used to Heath's deflections and ignored it.

"Your grades have been suffering a lot lately. You're failing four of your six classes and one of them is P.E. How do you fail P.E.?"

Heath fought off shame's desire to spread across his face and said, "I keep forgetting my uniform."

"Do you know what you want to do with your future, Heath?"

Pain silently struggled with shame, as Heath tried to maintain his composure. He was not about to give up his façade to either one.

"Yeah, I want to play football," he replied, finally finding the courage to meet his counselor's face.

Unlike Heath, Mr. Amara did not hide his emotions as pity entered his eyes.

"You know your injury has made that impossible."

"You asked me what I wanted to do," countered

Heath.

"Do you have a plan B?" asked Mr. Amara, thinking that they would need to invent extra letters for the alphabet before Heath got to the one that led him to success.

"Win the lottery," Heath replied.

"I really hope there's a plan C," Mr. Amara sighed.

Oddly enough, Heath had one.

"Sure. Go to college, drop out and then sell my body to science. What do you think I can get for half a brain and a bum arm?"

Mr. Amara rubbed his salt and pepper hair in frustration. He usually didn't let his students see that side of him because he knew some found satisfaction in that, but he was aware Heath was just as frustrated by the conversation as he was.

"I know you're upset about losing the scholarship to Michigan, but football isn't everything," said Mr. Amara, knowing his words weren't exactly consoling.

"But it is to me," Heath shot back. "Or it was. I don't know how to do anything else." It was the first time Heath had ever verbalized his feelings aloud and the words brought him anguish. It reminded him of the day the doctor told him he would never be able to play organized football again.

"You're a good kid Heath. You have a lot of potential but flunking out during your senior year will definitely screw things up for you in the long run. Talk to your teachers about extra credit. Get those grades up and we'll figure out the rest later." Mr. Amara regretted his words immediately. Heath was not a stupid kid, yet in the few minutes he had with him, he reminded him of everything going wrong in his life. He knew that if given time, Heath would realize he was more than just a jock.

Heath stood up and muttered, "Whatever." He felt as if one more person had just thrown another wooden plank onto the bonfire of his future. As Heath was walking out of the counselor's office, his cell phone vibrated signaling that he had received a text message. He took out his phone to read it and saw it was from Mike. The message read: *Can't take you to get your car. Have to work. Sorry.*

"Unbelievable," he muttered under his breath as he walked towards the next class he was failing.

With his book-bag slung on his back, Heath walked past storefronts, on his way to the mechanic's shop to get his car. It had been in the shop for the last three days to have its radiator replaced. As hot and tired as he was, he kept reminding himself that getting his car back would make things better. It always did. Even after the accident. Up until last year, Heath had two loves: football and his motorcycle. Football was going to take him to college and hopefully the NFL. But his motorcycle took him everywhere else until last March when he lost control taking a tight curve he had taken hundreds of times before. He tore two muscles in his rotator cuff, and his throwing arm was never the same even with surgery. That one accident cost him his two passions. Just like his arm, he swore that bike would never be whole again. Football was no longer an option and as soon as he was released from the hospital, he took what was left of his bike and finished what the crash had started. He took the refuse and dropped it off at several junkyards and dump sites around the city.

As soon as he was ready to drive again, his dad gave him a black 1970 Plymouth Barracuda. Though he had been out of the hospital for several months by then, he didn't feel he had truly started to heal until the moment he sat down in the front seat of his car. When things became overwhelming or stressful, he would drive aimlessly for hours and right now, he really needed it. At that moment, Heath was lost in thought about his car and the storefronts. He never paid much attention to the stores that were here since he was usually speeding past them. To him, they were usually just a really long blur. But now that he had to actually walk past them, he took the time to read their names. If it sounded interesting, he would peek inside only to be let down. *Sigh.* It just wasn't the mall.

Heath suddenly stopped where he stood and stared into the antique store he was just about to pass. It wasn't the *Old is New Again Antiques* name that got his attention but the pretty red head inside who was standing behind a glass counter. Heath walked into the store trying to appear as nonchalant as possible as if the smell of rosin and wood cleaner was nothing new to him.

Can't be too obvious he thought to himself but quickly realized that his attempt was futile. How many eighteen-year-olds walk into antique shops? He thought he should at least pretend to be interested in the archaic furniture or ancient knickknacks, but he just couldn't understand why anyone would want to buy old stuff, and didn't bother with browsing. The pretty shop girl smiled at him nonetheless and seemed to give the impression she knew him.

"Hey," he said when he reached the counter, trying not to stare at her ruby lips.

"Hi," she replied in return.

Heath was desperately trying to think of something clever to say but ended up with, "Anything good?" Maybe he would seem more convincing if he actually looked around the store but he couldn't take his eyes off her striking face.

She continued smiling, blushed a little and said. "A few things but they're really pricey. Were you looking for anything in particular?"

He was too tired to continue his charade.

"Not really. I just wanted to get your number," he admitted, mesmerized by her freckles and rare beauty.

Her smile broadened in spite of his confession

and said, "I appreciate your honesty. I'm Sarah Hughes."

Heath's smile grew as big as hers when he said, "I'm Heath."

"I know," she said, surprising him. She was a freshman at their school but she wasn't about to admit that. She was also not going to tell him how she shoved students out of her way just to catch glimpses of him in the crowded hallway when they were switching to their fifth period classes. So what could she say? "We go to the same school."

Heath racked his brain trying to remember if he'd ever passed by her in the hallways or shared a class but came up empty.

"We do? How come I've never seen you before?"

Her smile lessened as if slightly embarrassed and said, "We've never had any classes together and I come here after school to help my parents run the store."

"Oh. Well, what are my chances of getting your number?"

She hesitated for a moment before saying, "Not too good. I've seen you hanging around Amber Sullivan." It turned out Amber was a pain in his rear even when she wasn't around.

"Then you would also know that she's a junior who thinks we're together. We're just friends."

"With benefits?" Sarah asked.

"Only if you consider whining and nagging benefits."

Sarah eyed him for a moment. He could tell she wanted to believe him.

"Do you have a pen?" she finally asked.

Woo hoo.

Heath reached into his book bag to take out a pen, but couldn't find it. He gave up his futile search after unzipping and searching its various compartments.

"I must have lost it," he said, mostly to himself.

Sarah smiled and said, "I think I have one."

She rummaged around the cash register but couldn't find the blue pen she thought she had seen earlier. She remembered that a gentleman had stopped by an hour ago to sell a box-shaped anniversary clock with a beveled glass dome, a set of crystal candlesticks and a few other unimportant knick knacks she thought her father had paid too much for. The man had used her pen to sign the bill of sale and she guessed he accidentally left with it but then realized her good fortune. One of the items her father had also bought off the man was a gilded red herringbone fountain pen currently on display in the glass counter. She slid open a small counter door and removed the fountain pen from the top shelf. She then grabbed a business card from the top of the counter and wrote her phone number on the back of the card. Sarah smiled and handed the card and the pen to Heath. He held out the pen back to Sarah.

"This is yours," he reminded her.

But she only smiled and said, "Keep it. It's just a

stupid pen." Her father never concerned himself too much with the items in the cabinet and she knew it would be months before he ever realized it was gone. Besides, they were making her work the night of the big football game and felt she had the right to give away a parting gift to the school's former football star.

Heath smiled appreciatively at her and said, "Thanks."

As he was putting away the pen and the card which now had a phone number he actually wanted to call, Sarah told Heath, "Call me sometime."

With those words of encouragement, Heath replied, "Definitely." Heath walked out of the store, silently thanking his car for coming through for him yet again.

3
A Matter of Time

Heath was beyond exultant as soon as he pulled up his car in the school parking lot. It had been a long time since he had felt this excited. The feeling reminded him of his childhood, on nights before Christmas morning. It didn't matter that he was on his way to first period and it was only Tuesday. He had his car back and the hottest girl in Fort Lauderdale had given him her number.

Forget the three day rule, he thought to himself as he was walking to his class. *I might just call her later today.*

He searched the diverse faces in the hallways hoping he might even run into Sarah but his natural high quickly dissipated when he came across a poster advertising the regional final championship that was scheduled for later that evening. High school football usually ended in December but due to several hurricane threats in September and October, a few games had to be pushed back by four weeks. He stopped to stare at the glorified image of the school's current quarterback, and wished it were him in the picture and not Jim Harris.

What a tool, he thought as a stream of students brushed past him.

The hallway seemed to shrink as Carlos Torres, a colossal linebacker, walked up to Heath while he was lost in envy. When Heath finally acknowledged the giant's presence, he noticed that Carlos was wearing his navy blue jersey with the number eleven printed on the front and an angry looking crane, dive-bombing on the sleeves. Heath aimed some of his envy at the imposing boy next to him, who would be playing in today's big game.

"Are you going tonight?" Carlos asked innocently. Ever since the accident, Heath had not attended a single game and Carlos hoped that today would be the exception. For once, Heath was actually grateful he had a valid reason to skip out on yet another one.

"I'm not sure. I have a lot homework." Even though he had told the truth, Heath had as much trouble believing it as Carlos did.

"Since when do you do homework?" he asked with disbelief.

"Since I might not graduate," Heath admitted.

"That sucks," Carlos replied. "Where're you going now?"

"Algebra Two," Heath said, dreading his next class.

"In the portables?" Carlos asked, clearly repulsed. Heath understood Carlos's reaction. He hated the small classrooms, even if the portables were brand new. They were brought in to help deal with the ever-growing student population but Heath thought they were just as bad as the uniform policy the school had adopted three years ago.

"Yeah. It's so annoying. I'm always late." Only a sadist could have created his schedule. Why else would his language arts class and his math class be as far away from each other as possible, with only five minutes to get to class on time? One more tardy and he would get Saturday detention.

"Then you better hurry cause the bell is about to ring." Heath could swear Carlos was smiling mischievously as he walked away and entered a nearby classroom. Heath rushed for the doorway that lead outside to the portables and swore under his breath when the bell rang just as he reached it.

Heath sat impatiently in his Algebra II class as his teacher, Mr. Davis was explaining how to find the variable in a linear expression to the class and writing what looked like gibberish on the board.

Could this man be any duller, he thought to himself angrily, thinking about the detention slip tucked away in his back pocket.

Mr. Davis's gray hair, wrinkled skin, and absentmindedness screamed geriatric. Heath had had him as a teacher two years in a row now, and the man still couldn't get Heath's name right. Heath just sat there, bored, counting down until the bell rang.

"You know, Keith, you might actually learn something if you took the time to take notes."

Mr. Davis's voice brought Heath out of his stupor. It annoyed him to get singled out like that considering nearly half the students in the class either had the hoods of their sweaters pulled over their heads so that they could conceal the headphones of their MP3 players or rested their heads on their desks as they quietly napped like pimpled faced monks who had taken an oath of sleep, only waking up long enough to sneak out a few text messages. The only other students who were forced to remain conscious in class, sat in the two rows in front of Heath and were within range of Mr. Davis's failing eyesight.

Heath rolled his eyes as he reached for his book bag and took out a yellow spiral notebook and the pen Sarah gave him the day before. He opened the notebook to a blank page, wrote his name at the top of the paper and right underneath that, wrote the date but as soon as he had finished writing it, he realized he had written the wrong year. Before he could correct it, he heard scribbling and everything around him suddenly disappeared, including the desk he was sitting in, and he fell to the ground.

When Heath regained his senses, he looked around him and saw he was sitting in an empty field of wet grass with his notebook lying beside him; the same field where the portables used to be.

"What the hell just happened?" he asked himself. As much as he had always dreamed of the school burning down or disappearing, he never imagined his friends still inside when it happened. But the school hadn't disappeared, it was still there.

Where did the portables go?

He picked up his notebook and got to his feet. Blades of moist, cut grass stuck to him as if magnetized and he brushed them off his pants.

When did it rain?

The sultry air was thick with humidity and when he looked up, the sky seemed to be teasing to part its gray curtains for an encore. He walked around the field but he couldn't find any evidence that the classrooms ever existed. Not even portable-shaped impressions in the wet ground. He considered invisibility but he had seen enough science-fiction movies to realize he would have bumped into one of them by now, but it hadn't happened. He walked up to the school, hoping he would find someone who could help him. Men in white coats would be preferable. But when he got to the building, something odd caught his eye. There was a large aluminum bulletin board with cracked shatter-proof windows, secured to the main building's wall. The board was used to promote all upcoming school activities and among the various, colorful flyers, was a poster for a football game that took place over a year ago. A game he played in. He stared at his image that was grinning back at him from the poster, inviting everyone to watch Heath Wells and the Cranes whoop up on the Cobras.

That's impossible. Who would be that stupid or cruel?

But everything posted on the board advertised events that had just happened before or were about to happen in January of last year.

His heart beating like a trapped miner desperate to find a way out, Heath removed his phone from his front pocket and rummaged through his mind who he should call first. Just as he had settled on contacting his dad, he looked at his phone's screen and noticed the date. Even his phone had lost its mind because according to the device, the year was two-thousand thirteen. As much as he would like for it to be a practical joke, he knew that none of his friends had the know-how to tamper with the date and time on a cell phone.

He looked at his notebook where he had written the wrong year. He looked back up at the poster and then back at his phone, trying to make sense of his predicament. Heath realized they all had the same year. He looked again at his notebook and wrote the date again, this time writing it with the correct year. Nothing happened.

What if I...

He crossed out the wrong date and suddenly he heard the scribbling sound again. The portables seemed to rematerialize right before his eyes.

"Whoa," he said incredulously. He needed to sit down. So he did what he thought would be a good idea and went back to class.

Heath opened the door to his algebra II class and walked inside. Mr. Davis was still writing equations on the board. Not to Heath's surprise, the teacher hadn't noticed his sudden absence. He looked at Heath dismissively.

"Where are you coming from Keith?" asked the baffled teacher. Heath ignored the fact that Mr. Davis got his name wrong for the millionth time as he wracked his brain for a believable lie.

"Uh…the bathroom," he responded nervously, hoping the teacher wouldn't notice he was holding his notebook in his hand. He quickly scanned the room to see if anyone in the class would challenge his fib but everyone was either busy with class work, still asleep or deviously texting from their cell phones.

"When did I let you go the bathroom?" Mr. Davis questioned. It seemed the teacher was asking himself but Heath chose to answer him anyway.

"Don't you remember? I asked you a few minutes ago." Mr. Davis looked at Heath for a moment. It wasn't the first time he had forgotten something like that.

"Oh. Well then, go find your seat."

Relieved, Heath walked back to his desk, sat down and let out a giant sigh as he stared at the pen. He started to dwell on what had just happened, trying to piece together a bizarre puzzle. After a few minutes, he felt confident he had sorted most of it out. As crazy and impossible as it seemed, even though he had experienced it himself, Heath had traveled back in time. One year, to be exact. The reason the portables had disappeared was because they did not exist back then. They were installed over the summer just in time for the new school year. And most importantly, he was positive it was because of the pen. As Heath continued to mull his brief adventure, he was oblivious to the girl sitting behind him who stared at the back of his head with a perplexed expression on her face.

Heath sat on his bed, staring at the pen which rested on his untidy desk. His television was on but held no interest for him; especially now that the six o'clock news was airing. He finally got off his bed and walked over to the pen. He touched it briefly but then pulled back his hand in fear, as if it might bite him.

"This is crazy," he said to himself. "I did not just go back in time. It's a delayed reaction from the concussion I got last year."

He considered calling Sarah but not to ask her out. He wanted to know if she knew about the pen. But he didn't know what was more frightening: if she knew nothing about it or if she knew all along. Then something scarier than both those thoughts occurred to him.

What if she wanted the pen back?

His anxiety was finally distracted by a voice on the television. He looked up at the small flat screen, perched on his dresser to see one of the toothy newscasters making an interesting announcement for once.

"We would like to remind our viewers to play the lottery before tomorrow night's drawing. The current jackpot for the Powerball is one-hundred and fifty million dollars. Good luck everyone."

Heath looked back at the pen on the desk and smiled.

Heath stood in the darkened alleyway of a strip mall, clutching the pen and a piece of paper. The stench of rotting food still warm from the sun, nearly overwhelmed him. He could see the rear entrances for the dry cleaners that ruined one of his mom's favorite dresses and the liquor store where many of his friends somehow managed to get alcohol. But his point of interest was further down the alley. He surveyed the area several times making sure no one was around before he carried out his plan. As he looked around, he only saw trash littered on the floor and bins overflowing with garbage bags. When he was positive that it was just him and the smell of compost in the alley, he wrote a date on the piece of paper that was two days from his present. He heard the expected scribbling sound but didn't notice any changes. When he glanced around again, he noticed subtle differences. The trash on the floor was scattered differently as if someone had tried to redecorate. He also noticed that the trash bins now had less trash bags. He remembered Thursday was garbage day and assumed it had been collected earlier in the day. Heath walked out of the alleyway and made his way to the Food Spot located towards the opposite end of the strip mall.

He approached the young store clerk and nervously asked, "Do you know what last night's winning numbers were?"

The convenience store clerk, who had barely graduated from high school two years ago, appeared to be inconvenienced by Heath's presence and then pointed at the large numbers displayed on the even larger sign.

One, three, twelve, thirteen, fifteen and twenty-five, Heath repeated to himself, as he committed the numbers to memory. He hoped he didn't forget them when he got back to Tuesday.

This is insane.

Heath placed the lottery ticket with the winning numbers on his desk. He hated that he had to let time pass naturally before he could claim his prize but he knew he had no choice. Yet he vibrated with excitement and not just because was going to wake up a multi-millionaire in two days but because he was finally aware of the possibilities.

The things I could see. The places I could go, he thought excitedly.

He sat at his desk and opened his American history book, hoping he would find something inspiring. But after a few minutes of flipping insipid page after even more insipid page, he slammed the book shut.

"Forget that. I'm failing history."

Heath noticed the sports section of the newspaper on the corner of his desk. The headline that caught his interest read: *Will the Super Bowl Still Matter in Fifty Years?*

"Fifty years, huh?" Heath considered the potential for traveling into the future and witnessing events everyone else would have to wait for. He thought about all the bets he would make and never lose. He picked up the pen and said, "Let's find out. Twenty sixty- four, here I come." He wrote his intended travel date on a piece of paper but nothing happened. No scribbling sound, no subtle deviations in his room. Everything remained exactly the same and he assumed that included today's date. Heath tried writing a few more future dates, close to the fifty-year mark he was trying to reach, without success. Confused, he held the pen closely to his face and asked it, "Why aren't you working anymore?"

4
Timeline

Heath sat at the crowded cafeteria table as Mike, some of his former teammates, which he hardly spoke to lately, and Amber chatted away loudly about things Heath could only assume were trivial at best. Lunch was usually his favorite time of the school day because sometimes a few girls would join their group and argue over which popular, young male celebrity he resembled most. Heath knew he could never be confused for any of the stars they compared him to but he still enjoyed the attention. Today, it didn't matter who anyone thought he resembled. He was detached from the day's usual juvenile shenanigans.

It was Wednesday, which meant everyone in the school, including the faculty, was excited that they were halfway through the week. His friends were all caught up in talking and laughing which was an entertaining web that Heath usually got tangled up in as well, but today was different. He was still stuck on yesterday.

Why didn't it work?

The problem confounded him but his friends were oblivious to his troubled ruminations. He took a bite out of his half eaten pizza and then placed it back on his black foam tray, while his chocolate milk remained untouched. Even though he usually thought that cafeteria food tasted like vomit after binging on tofu and oatmeal, something else had stolen his appetite. He finally shoved the tray away from him, sliding it silently across the gray table and glanced over at Amber who happened to be staring at him but he knew it wasn't out of concern.

What the hell… He needed to talk to someone.

He leaned over and in a low voice asked, "What do you know about time travel?"

Amber looked at him for a moment trying to determine if he was joking or actually serious. She finally decided she didn't care because he was talking to her. She gave the question some thought until a very dim light bulb went off in her head.

"Easy. It's traveling through time."

Slightly frustrated Heath tried to coax a better answer from her.

"Do you know anything else?" he asked.

"I know that if you go back in time, you'll meet your mother, she'll fall in love with you and you'll never be born. Why? Do you have a Delorean?" she asked excitedly.

She was hurt and confused when he mumbled, "Never mind," and turned his attention to his friends at the table.

Someone from their table stood up and Heath saw that it was Mike, who was holding an apple in his hand with a mischievous grin on his face. He followed Mike's line of sight and saw he was staring at the table across from theirs where a lone female student named

Aphrodite was sitting. Heath sensed what Mike was up to and looked forward to whatever it was he had in mind for the most reviled girl in school.

Was she even a girl?

Heath had known Aphrodite for years but unlike moss, she did not grow on him or his friends. She was wearing her typical outfit which consisted of a black, over-sized polo shirt and baggy khaki pants. Clothing that seemed unwilling to touch her either. Even though the school uniform also included white and navy blue shirts to choose from, he had never seen her wearing any other color than black and wondered if she owned several black tops or just the one shirt.

He didn't think she or anyone else had ever tried to put a brush to her hair. It was a mess of mane that a family of squirrels would find inviting. It was a long, dark, frizzy disaster. As for her face, the copious amounts of acne would be enough to challenge even the most gifted dermatologist. And worst of all, she sat behind Heath in his algebra II class which made it doubly torturous. She was often the object of their much deserved cruelty and it was a hobby they had all come to enjoy. Heath kept watching the pathetic figure at the table, anxious for Mike's assault. Suddenly, the apple Mike had been holding went whizzing through the air and landed in a bowl of chocolate pudding on Aphrodite's tray. Heath's table erupted with laughter and applause while Aphrodite jumped in shock. She appeared dismayed from the chocolaty chaos Mike had inflicted.

Mike shouted, “Three points!” and high-fived everyone at the table.

Amber screeched, “Geek goddess!” which drew a fresh round of laughter.

Aphrodite shot the members of their table a dirty look, which only amused them further. Heath couldn’t understand her annoyance. It’s not like anyone would be able to see the pudding stains on her shirt.

Heath then saw something that made him stop laughing. As Aphrodite cleaned off the chocolate, she propped up a soft-covered book on the table, to wipe some of the mess off it. The book that suddenly captured his attention was called, *The Time Traveler’s Wife*. A strange combination of revulsion and hope began to build up in Heath.

After the last bell of the day died out, Heath stalked Aphrodite through the school’s labyrinth of blue dilapidated lockers and hallways. At first, he kept his distance because he didn’t want anyone to see them together but as the hallways cleared out, he also feared being alone with her. He kept his distance until he finally found the courage to call out her name.

“Aphrodite,” he said hopefully loud enough for only her to hear but she continued walking as if she hadn’t heard him. “Aphrodite!” he called out louder. By this time, he had caught up to her and she suddenly wheeled around to face him.

"I'm sorry. Were you trying to get my attention?" she asked with contempt. "Maybe you should have thrown an orange at the back of my head."

Even though Heath knew she would be upset, he wasn't prepared to handle this, a cornered animal ready to attack without hesitation.

"That wasn't me," he blurted sheepishly. He was trying desperately not to stare at the blots of chocolate, peeking out from her hair.

"You're still a jerk," she snarled, glaring at him with her burning dark eyes which reminded him of a shark; black, unblinking and menacing. For a brief moment, a look came over her face as if she wanted to say something else but it melted away and left an angry glare.

"I know I deserve that, but I'm not looking to fight with you," he said in a feeble attempt to be nice but she continued to stare angrily at him. "Or insult you," he added quickly.

"Oh good. God must like me today," she responded sarcastically.

Remembering why he was speaking to her, Heath said, "I noticed that book you were reading."

Aphrodite's eyes narrowed and she held up the book, tempted to smack him in the head with it.

"You mean this book?"

"Yes," he replied, thinking they were finally understanding each other but instead, rage returned to her eyes.

"The same book I've been holding to my face for the last three years hoping everyone would ignore me?"

Heath was confused.

"You mean you've never actually read it?"

"Does reading eighty pages count? You guys never leave me alone long enough to actually finish it."

This is hopeless, he thought, but then got another idea.

"It doesn't matter. I'm writing a story for English and I need help with it."

Aphrodite looked at him incredulously and asked, "Why would I help you?"

She couldn't believe his audacity. Well, actually she could. He was the type of person who trips you on the floor and then asks you to pick up something they dropped while you're down there. He was as heartless and brainless as a…well as a high-school jock. She chuckled to herself but then she remembered she was speaking to Heath Wells and her humor disappeared like sunlight during an eclipse.

Heath knew that if he said the wrong words to her, she would bolt and he would be back to square one. He decided to appeal to her good side… if she had one.

"Because deep down inside you're a decent person, a better person than me."

She knew he was being insincere but she was intrigued by their exchange. Why would someone who despised her and usually only spoke to her to insult her, suddenly need her help?

"What about all those terrible things you've said about me?" she asked.

"Peer pressure? My mother never hugged me enough... No?"

By the look on her face, Heath could tell she was unimpressed so he decided to be honest for once.

"I'm a jerk. All I can do is apologize for being a jerk. I don't think that's going to help you much."

Surprised by his candor, Aphrodite lowered her guard just a bit.

"I'm so stupid," she said under her breath. "What's the story?"

Heath was nervous about saying the words aloud.

"It's about..." he leaned close to her and whispered, "time travel."

Aphrodite looked at him quizzically and asked, "Why are you whispering?" *And people think I'm weird*, she thought.

Heath wasn't sure if he wanted to continue the conversation but he was desperate for answers.

"I need to know why someone who could travel into the future, no longer can." Aphrodite now looked at him as if he were less crazy and actually gave his proposed dilemma some thought.

"Simple. The machine is broken." But her response only frustrated Heath.

"No, it's not broken. It's…" he caught himself before he revealed more than he wanted. "You know what? Forget about it."

Heath walked away leaving a baffled Aphrodite in the empty corridor.

Aphrodite propped herself across the black fleece blanket that she had laid out across the wooden floor. Actually, it was a Snuggie her parents had given her a few Christmases ago, thinking she would love it because it had a Jack Skellington print but Aphrodite never used it with that purpose because she refused to wear a dress, no matter the pattern. She knew they loved her but she felt they didn't know her at all.

They were so oblivious, she was convinced that should either one of them suddenly develop leprosy, they would think they had a really bad rash. As much as she had tried to explain to them why she had no social life or friends, they would insist that it was because she was shy and needed to smile more often. She assumed their cluelessness stemmed from the fact that they became parents late in life and she was their only child. Their intentions were well meaning but were still annoying. That was why she escaped almost every night to be by herself in her secret hideaway. She was there now finishing up her homework.

A stack of glossy college pamphlets sat at her side. They were from various universities located in the northernmost parts of the United States. She had no idea what she was going to study and it didn't matter to her. She just wanted to take the college fund her grandmother had set aside for her and get as far away from Florida as she could. The idea of being snowed in and isolated from the rest of the world was becoming more enticing every day.

As she toiled away on the last of the math problems, she thought about Heath's assignment. She had to admit she was intrigued and wished her English teacher would give her really cool writing topics as well. After a few moments, Aphrodite realized it was almost ten o'clock and didn't want to risk falling asleep on the floor. She had done it in the past a few times and every time she would wake up with back pain that lasted the whole day and required medicinal pain relief to get rid of. As she gathered her books and blanket from the floor, she thought about her comfortable bed, Heath's story and a lingering notion that seemed to be trying to claw its way out of her brain.

5
It's About Time

The following day, Heath and Aphrodite sat in their usual seats in their algebra II class, neither one of them paying attention to Mr. Davis's lesson on quadratics. For the first time since the school year started, Aphrodite leaned over to speak to Heath. Odder than that was when Heath leaned slightly back in his seat to listen.

In a hushed tone, Aphrodite told him, "I've been thinking about your story."

Her words brought him anxiety and not just because he feared someone would notice them conversing.

"And?..." he asked nervously. Aphrodite misread his tension, assuming he was reacting to her proximity and relished it because she was making him suffer for a change. It was a shame this conversation was already almost over.

"The easiest explanation is there is no future." Aphrodite settled back into her seat while Heath wanted to jump out of his.

Heath sat motionless in his car which was idling in the school parking lot. The engine had been running for the last ten minutes, but he couldn't bring himself to put the car into drive. His thoughts were tumbling inside his mind but each one was a clone of the original, there is no future. He was startled when he heard a knock on his driver's side window. It was Aphrodite.

He heard her muffled voice when she asked, "What's your damage?"

He lowered the window an inch with the manual crank, and as coolly as possible replied, "I don't know what you're talking about." But he then discovered one more reason to dislike Aphrodite. She was stubborn.

"I helped you with your stupid story but you walked out of class like I told you were dying of cancer."

He didn't need this right now.

"You're seeing things," he said dismissively.

Words suddenly materialized on Aphrodite's tongue. The same words she wanted to say to Heath the day before but was afraid to because she already felt foolish covered in chocolate pudding. This time, she had to ask.

"Does this have something to do with the other day?"

Heath's poker face was compromised by her words.

Crap. "What other day?" he asked hoping to sound innocent but instead sounded suspicious.

Doubt crept into Aphrodite's voice as she replied, "Never mind."

But before she could walk away, Heath opened his car door to confront her. He had to know.

"What other day?" he demanded as he got out of

his car.

Aphrodite refused to be intimidated by some stupid jock, even if he was over six feet tall and her black Converse shoes didn't add much to her five-foot-five figure.

She looked him in the eyes and said, "The other day, when we were sitting in class. I didn't exactly see anything but I could tell that one moment you were sitting in front of me and then you weren't."

"I got up to go to the bathroom."

"No, you didn't," she countered.

"But you just admitted you didn't see anything."

"I know what I didn't see," she said, feeling foolish.

"So you think I disappeared?" he asked in mock disbelief.

"Yes," she replied, maintaining her ground.

"That's insane. It's…it's…" his words trailed off as if the wind had swept them away. It was pointless arguing any further.

"It's true, isn't it?" she asked, her voice tinged with relief.

Heath nodded his head silently in defeated affirmation. Then something rarer than the appearance of Haley's Comet occurred when a smile streaked across Aphrodite's face.

"Oh, thank God! I thought I was losing my mind. How did you do it?"

Heath studied her for a moment. He was still in shock from their exchange but also relieved that he finally had someone he could confide in.

But why did it have to be her?

Reluctantly, Heath turned around and reached for his book bag that was set on the passenger side seat. Aphrodite heard a zipper unzipping and when Heath faced her again, he was holding a red pen. He held it up and waved it.

Confused, she said, "I don't understand."

"It's a time machine," he confessed. And just as he had expected from anyone he admitted this to, she looked at him as if he were insane.

"No. That's a pen..."

"...that takes you through time," he insisted.

Aphrodite was convinced he was trying to prank her and at any moment his friends would appear, laughing as they succeeded in humiliating her once again.

She turned, and as she walked away she said, "I think the damage to your arm has inexplicably traveled to your so-called brain."

Heath caught up to her, grabbed her arm and wheeled her around to face him. Now that he had a confidant, even if it was Aphrodite, he wasn't about to let her go.

"I'm serious. Let me show you."

It seemed that ever since Heath came into possession of the pen, his life had become a series of bizarre events. He just couldn't decide what was the most peculiar; traveling through time or driving Aphrodite to his house and sitting next to her on his bed. He was leaning towards the latter.

At least he didn't have to worry about having to come up with a lame reason to explain her presence to his family. His parents wouldn't be back from work for another two hours and his brother usually stopped by his girlfriend's house after school.

He was holding the pen as he explained, "The way it works is you write down a date and it takes you there."

Although Aphrodite usually had reason to distrust Heath, she believed him. It explained his Houdini act from the other day.

"Where did you go that day we were in class?"

He smiled as he briefly relived the moment in his head, recalling, "I went back one year exactly."

Intrigued, she wanted to know more about his experiences with the pen.

"What about the future?"

Heath's face became grave.

"I was able to travel two days ahead but when I tried to go fifty years, it wouldn't work." Aphrodite began to understand Heath's reaction in class.

"And now you think I'm right."

"What else could it be?" he asked anxiously.

"Maybe it has limitations," she suggested. "Maybe fifty years is too far ahead. You said yourself you only went back one year. Maybe that's the max."

Heath considered her words but decided that if he told her the whole truth, she would understand his despair.

"I have this strange feeling that it's not that. A fortune teller told me that something terrible was going to happen and I would be involved."

"And I get to be a witness? Oh goody!" she said sardonically. She scanned his room quickly, looking for anything humiliating to use against him later but she was disappointed to discover that aside from the messy desk littered with old homework and stacks of failed exams, she had no ammunition. Not even a childhood teddy in sight.

"I could use more ideas and less sarcasm."

"Then let's run a test, "she suggested. " Pick a day that's more than one year in the future. Let's say...five years from today and see what happens."

Deciding that her idea had merit, Heath walked over to his desk, sat down and grabbed a piece of paper to write his travel date but when Aphrodite realized what he was about to do, she ran over to him and snatched the paper away.

"What are you doing?" she asked with alarm.

Confused, he replied, "I'm going to try for five

years." But this only distressed her further.

"Are you crazy? You can't do that in your room. What if the you in five years is here when you pop in? You could create a time paradox. You're going to have to find somewhere neutral."

Heath looked at her confused and insulted.

"A time what? And what makes you think I'll still be living here in five years?" Aphrodite couldn't decide between listing her reasons in alphabetical order or just naming the obvious but then realized either one would take all day.

"What makes you think you won't?" she said finally.

"I have a plan," he answered cagily.

"Whatever," she said dismissively. "We need a different location."

"What did you have in mind?" he inquired.

Aphrodite looked at him, a smile tugging at the left corner of her mouth.

6
Time Frame

Heath and Aphrodite stood quietly, staring at the old Bailey House, mostly because it was an odd structure for the suburbs. Heath didn't know much about architecture but he had seen enough houses to realize it didn't belong in the neighborhood, or anywhere else in the United States. The light colored house's pink glow mirrored the sky's crimson highlights, created by the sun's slow decent into oblivion. Heath had heard about the famous edifice but had never taken the time to search for it in its hidden cul-de-sac, which was obscured by tall, neatly trimmed hedges. The two-story stone and stucco home, with its arched doorway and windows, looked like a country abode one would find tucked between the rural, rolling hills of France.

Aphrodite brought him out of his trance when she grabbed his arm and announced, "Let's go." But Heath refused to follow until he had more answers.

"Why are we here?"

Aphrodite's black-marble eyes rolled in her head as if she was about to explain the reason for the millionth time.

"Because we need a location that will still be here several years from now and this is a historically protected landmark. It's perfect."

"How are we getting in?" he challenged.

"Follow me," she said, motioning with her right hand. They both walked to the back of the house. Aphrodite walked up to a large window and then slid it open.

"How did you know it was open?" Heath asked with surprise.

"I came here on a tour once and unlocked it when no one was looking," she answered in a matter of fact tone. Heath looked at her askance. "I like to come here when I need to escape," she added defensively.

Heath followed Aphrodite through the open window and found himself in a pitch-black space. He froze where he stood, afraid of tripping over any unseen objects.

"It's pretty dark in here," he remarked.

"Kind of like your soul."

Heath ignored the quip as he listened to the patter of Aphrodite's feet while she navigated the murky room effortlessly. He heard the soft click of a light switch, which revealed a spacious kitchen with pale yellow cabinets and red brick walls. He followed Aphrodite into the next dim room where another light switch chased the shadows away. They were in a furnished living room where Heath could swear the old moss green sofa with the cerise floral print had absorbed the various scents of everyone who had ever sat there. Old pictures were scattered across the walls like a disorganized parade. There was a walnut colored display case against the wall whose main attraction seemed to be a few old tools and a mantle with an ugly brown vase. He made his way around the dimly lit room, the wooden floors groaning with every step. The faded, floral wallpaper, which was peeling at the corners, seemed to be begging to be removed. He glanced at the odd curios and photos of nameless faces, trying to understand how the house warranted perpetual protection.

"Why is this house so important, anyway?" he inquired.

Aphrodite sighed deeply, recalling the tour guide's speech she had overheard at least twenty times, while hiding out in the attic upstairs.

In a very unenthusiastic, almost robotic voice, she recited, "Henry Bailey was a renowned architect who traveled to Europe every year with his darling wife, Sylvia. Their adventures tragically came to an end when Sylvia was diagnosed with breast cancer. In his undying love for her, he built this home, which is an exact replica of her favorite house in Normandy. Sadly, Sylvia Bailey passed away before the project was completed but Henry continued his devoted endeavor. He passed away a few months later, when the house was finished. The Bailey house is not only a work of art but of enduring love as well."

Heath shrugged his shoulders and admitted, "I still don't understand why this house is important."

"I don't either," she agreed. "I think it's because it's really old and a president visited here once but I mostly think the tourists come to see the dead people."

Those last words startled Heath who anxiously twisted in place expecting to be ambushed by one of the beloved Baileys.

"This house is haunted?" he asked horrified.

"Don't be stupid," she replied coldly. "They're in the urn on the mantle. It was his dying wish that they be together."

"Oh," he said, as he glanced at the brown object above the disused fireplace.

"Nice to know you're fearless," she said sarcastically. "Let me know if you want me to turn on the hall lights."

Feeling foolish, Heath followed Aphrodite to the attic.

Heath stood in the dusty attic, looking nervously at Aphrodite. The cramped space was littered with storage boxes and items he thought only existed in old movies such as the dressmaker's dummy wearing a simple, raw silk wedding dress whose original snowy material had yellowed over the years. It stood in a corner as if waiting for its lost love to return. The room smelled of turpentine and mothballs that reminded Heath of his grandparent's house. It was almost comforting.

"Are you sure this is a good idea?"

"It's perfect," she replied. "You can go as far ahead as you want without worrying about running into someone you don't want to, especially yourself. Are you ready?" she inquired as she held out the pen and a piece of paper to Heath.

He assented silently when he accepted the items from her. He wrote the agreed upon date on the piece of paper, heard the scribbling sound and popped out of existence.

Fighting the shock of watching someone disappear into thin air, Aphrodite tilted her wrist to view the silver face of her wide, black leather watch to time Heath but the second hand barely had a chance to tick off five seconds before he seemed to emerge from nothingness.

"That's it?" Aphrodite exclaimed. "You were only gone for a few seconds!"

"Aphrodite, I was there at least fifteen minutes," he said, showing her his digital watch which was now sixteen minutes ahead of hers.

"Really? That's so cool," she responded, truly astounded as she quickly grabbed his wrist to study his watch more closely.

"You think that's cool?" he asked, as he reclaimed his arm from her.

"You came back to the same time you left. That means you could be gone for years, come back and it would be like you never left. Well, except you might look older. What was it like?"

Heath searched her face for signs of insincerity but was surprised to find none.

"Um, nothing special. I didn't leave the house so I didn't see anything major."

Aphrodite seemed a little disappointed and looked away pensively.

"At least we know there's a future five years from now," she stated.

"But not in fifty," he reminded her.

Her mind must have been a maze of thoughts because it took Aphrodite a few moments before she spoke again.

"What if it's less than that?" she proposed.

"What do you mean?"

"We know it doesn't work for fifty years but what if there's no future after fifteen or even ten years?"

Heath realized the possibility and became alarmed.

"We have to do something!" he exclaimed. But to his surprise, Aphrodite did not share his concern.

"Are you kidding me? Life sucks. I want it to end, even if it might take a while," she scoffed. She sat down on a large cedar hope chest and stared at Heath defiantly. Not that she woke up every day wanting the world to end, but she was tired of being treated like a freshman at senior prom and she had also grown weary from the constant injustice that seemed to occur every two seconds in one place or another in the world. Sometimes she just felt that if the earth were to suddenly stop spinning, it wouldn't be such a bad thing.

Heath returned her gaze while his forgotten scorn for her attempted to hijack his tongue. Resorting to name-calling would get him nowhere, he realized. Aside from the fact that she would probably kill him, if everything they had hypothesized was correct, she might be the one person who could help him.

He regained his composure yet a dab of annoyance escaped his voice when he asked, "If it sucks so much, why haven't you killed yourself?"

Aphrodite's eyes darted to the right side of the room before she answered, oblivious of the disregarded stacks of storage boxes covered in a thick layer of dust and the cobwebs in the corner. Not that she was thinking of a believable lie but hesitant of telling him the truth.

She finally decided, what was one more laugh at her expense when the sweet relief of the apocalypse was around the corner.

Her eyes returned to Heath's face and she said, "Because it would be a sin and I refuse to die only to be transferred from one hell into another. It'll probably be like…high school." The last two words fell out of her mouth as if they were too sour to hold down.

But the moment she finished speaking, Heath found his loophole and announced, "Well then, now you have to help me."

"How do you figure that?" she challenged.

"Because you know people might die and it would be a sin if you let them," he said triumphantly.

"I could die before then," she countered.

"I don't know. You might have a long wait," he responded.

"A girl can dream, can't she?"

Heath heard defeat in her halfhearted retort. He also realized that he was an accomplice to her eagerness for the end of the world. All those years of verbal torture had left an empty soul whose only wish fulfillment was death.

His eyes softened as did his voice when he pleaded, "Help me figure out whatever the problem is before it happens and stop it from happening."

But Aphrodite's stare remained hard as she asked sarcastically, "How difficult could it possibly be for two teens who can't get along for more than five minutes to figure out perhaps a catastrophic crisis with a time travelling pen and fix it?"

Heath refused to let her bait his ire and calmly asked, "So we're just supposed to pretend we don't know anything and let it happen?"

"Not according to you but what can we do?"

"I was hoping you would know," he conceded.

Aphrodite stood up and began to pace the room, her face rapt with frustration.

"I'm not sure how useful I can be to you

considering it's a one passenger pen."

Heath looked at the paper in his hand and realized she was wrong.

"That might not be true. Whatever I've written the date on has come with me so..."

Aphrodite stopped where she stood and looked at Heath, as his idea penetrated her mind.

"One of us is going to have to be a calendar," she said, finishing his thought. "Wow. Your head isn't just for decoration," she added.

"Thanks," he said dryly. "Are you ready?"

Aphrodite's eyes bulged out of their sockets as if they wanted to escape Heath's really bad idea.

"You want to do this today?" she asked with shock. Heath didn't understand her reaction.

"Did you have a better day in mind?" he inquired.

"Not really, but we still don't know what day to go to."

"How do we figure that out?" Heath asked, hoping she had an answer he would like.

Aphrodite studied his face thoughtfully and asked, "Do you trust me?"

"Do I have a reason not to trust you?" he asked suspiciously.

She ignored his question and said, "Leave the pen with me for one day."

Of course her answer would totally suck, he

thought uneasily.

"I don't know," he said truthfully. "How do I know you won't do something that will cause me to have never been born?" Aphrodite looked away as if lost in a beautiful daydream. "Are you actually thinking about it?" he asked with distress. After all those years of bullying, he knew he couldn't blame her. Aphrodite returned from her musing and met his gaze with a wistful look in her eyes.

"You know I won't do that. We have a serious situation to deal with. I'll just have to erase you from existence another day."

"You're not exactly building trust here," he said exasperated. "What's to stop you from disappearing with the pen?"

Aphrodite sighed deeply. For some reason, providence decided for her to maybe save the world and gave her a coward for a sidekick.

"I promise to behave for the sake of all the puppies and rainbows in the world. And I will have a travel date for you by tomorrow," she said with as much sincerity as she could muster, which wasn't much.

Left without a choice, Heath handed the pen to her with trepidation.

7
Time's Up

On Friday morning, Heath walked into his Algebra II class hoping Aphrodite had a travel date just as she had promised. He began to wonder if recruiting her help would be considered cheating when Madam Souska had told him specifically that only he could prevent the impending catastrophe, but he decided he didn't care if it meant he didn't have to do it alone. But after a few minutes Heath realized fate might have other plans. Aphrodite never showed for class.

Maybe she's skipping, he thought to himself, but the heavy weight of unease seemed to have leased his stomach and was in no hurry to move out. He reminded himself that he would see her in the cafeteria during lunch. Nobody skips lunch. The class dragged on even longer than it usually did.

At lunch, Heath sat with his friends who were ignorant of his dismay. They never noticed that he wasn't participating in their playful banter, that he never touched his food, and that he stared at the empty table where Aphrodite should have been sitting.

Heath walked through the school corridors, trailed by a shadow of gloom. Did Aphrodite break her promise? Would he slowly fade away or would it be instantaneous?

How could I be so stupid?

He was absorbed in thought when Mike suddenly grabbed his arm and startled him. Mike thought it was funny that he gave Heath such a fright and cackled at his own assumed cleverness. Heath humored him with a phony chuckle. A thought occurred to Heath that gave him a sliver of hope.

"Hey, do you know where Aphrodite lives?" he asked tentatively. Mike's stupid grin disappeared and was replaced with a stupid scowl.

"No, why?" he asked.

Heath had to think fast. He didn't have time for the truth.

"Uh… I was thinking about egging her house later." Mike's face lit up as if Heath had given him a gift he had always wanted.

"Cool. Let me know if you find out and I'll bring the eggs." Mike made a fist with his right hand and held it up, signaling Heath to bump it with his. Heath mimicked Mike's gesture and bumped fists with him unenthusiastically. Mike smiled with satisfaction and walked away to his next class while Heath stood in the hallway desperately wondering where he could find Aphrodite.

Heath walked towards the back of the Bailey house and made his way to the unlocked window Aphrodite had shown him. The tours had ended an hour ago and he saw the caretaker lock up the house and leave so he knew it would be empty. Well, not completely empty, he hoped. The Bailey house was his last resort. If Aphrodite wasn't here, then he and the world were both doomed. He slid open the window and crawled inside. He closed the window behind him and made his way to the stairway.

Heath opened the attic door and scanned the room. He was stunned when he saw Aphrodite's listless body lying on the floor. His stomach dropped like a broken anchor.

He ran to her, yelling, "Aphrodite! Aphrodite!" and kneeled at her side.

Heath carefully rolled her over, terrified of having to confront her death stare but as soon as he had her on her back, Aphrodite sat up gasping like a swimmer desperate for air and shouted, "I swear Heath Wells kidnapped me and locked me up in here!" She craned her neck and met with Heath's bewildered gaze. "Oh, it's you," she said yawning. "What time is it?" she asked as she stretched her arms. Heath shook his head in disbelief.

"It's almost four," he answered as he stood back up. He noticed Aphrodite was dressed in a black Pink Floyd shirt and baggy jeans. He wondered if she had gone home to change or if she kept spare clothes in the attic.

She stopped stretching and looked at Heath in surprise.

"I missed school? Awesome," she expressed happily. She held out her hands to Heath who grabbed them and lifted her up to her feet. He assumed she was wearing the same clothes from the day before.

"You scared me for a minute there," he confessed.

This amused Aphrodite who asked, "You thought I skipped out with the pen, didn't you?"

"Well, that too, but when I came in, I thought you were dead." Aphrodite's mischievous smile evaporated and a frown appeared in its place.

"No such luck," she sighed. She bent down and picked up a paper off the floor. "I was up all night working on our little project," she said.

"And?" he asked with bated breath.

"We have a travel date," she announced confidently and held out a rumpled sheet of paper to Heath.

He took the paper from her and tried to decipher all the numbers and markings written in ink. He could see she had written several years on the paper. All of them were crossed out except her return date. But what caught his eye was the date with a star next to it and a lone date written in pencil.

"What does this mean?" he asked in confusion.

"The date with the star next to it is the last day

the pen will take you to. I'm guessing that's the day the world hits an iceberg." Heath gave her a quizzical look. "It's a metaphorical iceberg," she clarified. Heath nodded his head, pretending to understand. She pointed to the only date not written in ink and said, "The one that I wrote in pencil is a month before that."

"Why a month?" he asked curiously.

"I figure that it gets us close enough to the problem with enough time to fix it. And if we don't, we can always go back and try again," she said.

"What if we run out of ink?" Heath asked with concern. He wanted to save the future, not get stuck in it.

"We'll buy more," she said dismissively. But Heath wasn't satisfied with her solution.

"What if the magic's in the ink?" he challenged.

"Then we better get it right the first time," she admitted. "Or the second. I hope there's enough for a third," she trailed off, hoping the ink wasn't the flux capacitor.

"Sounds almost like a plan," he said halfheartedly. "So how far are we going?"

"Twenty-seven years."

Heath thought he heard a hint of excitement in her voice.

"So, twenty forty-one?"

"Yes," she replied, impressed he was able to do the math in his head.

"Does this mean we're ready to do this now?" he

asked expectantly.

"I guess," she said with a shrug.

Up until that moment, Heath's silent angst had been growing like a tumor in his stomach, because he didn't know how they were going to succeed in their assumed mission. Now, it seemed his fear was about to consume him because he wasn't sure if he was ready to take on this daunting task.

We're just a couple of kids, he thought to himself. The idea of trying to find someone more appropriate for the undertaking, convincing them of its magnitude, and then not only have them consent to it but succeed as well seemed beyond hopeless. He looked at Aphrodite who looked back at him curiously. He had to admire her for setting aside her hate for him to perhaps risk her life but then remembered she was suicidal.

Maybe this could be a win-win situation, he thought cynically.

"Should we prepare anything before we go?" he asked.

"What, like a picnic basket?" she asked derisively.

If she keeps this up, I'll be the genie that grants her death wish, he thought bitterly. Heath realized his endeavor was going to be painful on so many levels, starting with his time-traveling companion. Coincidentally, Aphrodite was having the same exact thought.

Heath let out a deep sigh and announced, "Let's do this."

Aphrodite removed the cap from the pen and began to write a date on Heath's arm.

She could feel Heath's body tense up as soon as she started writing and said, "Relax. It's not like I'm writing my phone number." Heath smiled slightly but the tension remained. Aphrodite was glad Heath couldn't see her face or he would have seen her fear.

We're too stupid to realize how stupid we are, she thought grimly and forced herself to finish writing out the date completely. They heard the scribbling sound and felt the pull on their bodies as they disappeared and reappeared in the Bailey attic.

They looked at each other dumbfounded, unsure if their plan had succeeded.

"Did it work?" he asked.

Staring at the attic doorway, Aphrodite responded, "There's only one way to find out."

8
Somewhere In Time

Heath and Aphrodite stood at the front doorway of the Bailey house, their faces fraught with tension, each one afraid of opening the door but not admitting it. Aphrodite looked over at Heath who was staring at the tarnished brass doorknob. She grabbed his right hand and placed it on the handle. Taking the hint, Heath turned the knob and slowly eased the door open.

Heath walked out first with Aphrodite trailing closely behind him, like a remora fish. They continued down the stone pathway, crossing the driveway and finally arriving at the main entrance of the cul-de-sac where it seemed the thick hedges were threatening to close in on them. The moment they stepped off the Bailey property, they both stood motionless as their eyes processed their new surroundings. Their mouths hung open like a couple of grinless dogs, their words shivered in their throats, afraid to be spoken. The neighborhood seemed to have been transformed into a vision right out of a futuristic science-fiction movie. The homes they were accustomed to seeing everyday were nearly unrecognizable in their modernized structure.

Three houses down from them, one of the neighbors stood in front of his home, painting its surface by simply pressing a button on a small remote he was holding. The house changed several hues until it finally stopped on a red and black plaid configuration that resembled a Scottish kilt. He smiled to himself as he slid the remote into his back pocket. He loved annoying his homeowner's association.

Sleek, ultramodern cars were either parked in driveways or quietly zipped through the streets, like predators stalking prey on an asphalt plain. Large copper plates, which Heath had assumed to be manhole covers, dotted the street curbside every few feet. They looked up as an airplane streaked across the sky as if shot out by a cannon.

Heath's stomach lurched momentarily when he didn't see his car parked on the curb, where he had left it. It seemed to settle down when he remembered he had left it in the year twenty-fourteen and hoped it wouldn't get stolen while he was gone.

"This is so surreal," Aphrodite gasped. Heath looked at her askew.

"So real?" he repeated incorrectly. "This is unreal!"

Aphrodite rolled her eyes, almost amused by his ignorance and said, "Come on scarecrow. Let's see if we can score you a brain." Aphrodite felt it would be best if they went into the city to seek information. She hoped it still existed where they had left it twenty-seven years ago. She turned left and followed the sidewalk. Heath followed her nervously, hoping she knew what she was doing because he sure didn't.

"Where are we going?" he finally asked.

"The city," she answered matter of fact. "I think that might be our…" Her words trailed off because at that moment, Aphrodite had stepped off the sidewalk to cross the street but instead of her foot finding blacktop, she stepped on one of the copper plates that seemed to sink beneath her weight. She was suddenly enveloped in a clear sphere. "What the…?" She punched futilely against the sides of the globe, which remained solid. She felt her stomach drop and realized with dismay that not only was she trapped in the sheer orb, it was rising into the air as if she had been made of helium.

Heath watched in horror as the one person he knew in the future slowly floated away.

Oh my God! "Aphrodite! Somebody help us! Aphrodite!" he yelled. His cries went unanswered as he ran after the sphere but he realized that it veered into a course that would be impossible to follow… on foot anyway. He looked around the neighborhood and spotted a cherry red motorcycle parked in one of the driveways. A lump of dread filled his stomach since he hadn't been on one since his accident a year ago. Despite his trepidation, he tossed his fear aside. His anxiety attack would just have to wait. He started to run towards the bike. It didn't look much different from the one he used to ride. He hoped the owner had left the key in the ignition but as soon as he mounted it, he saw that there was no key because there was no ignition switch. Where there should have been the instruments and indicators was just a small, flat screen.

This doesn't make any sense.

Lost in his bewilderment, Heath didn't notice when the owner of the confounding machine approached him. Heath started at the stranger's voice.

"Nice try guy, but you know that it only starts with an optical scan," said the man, pointing at the strange screen on the bike.

"Optical scan?" Heath asked with confusion.

"My eyes," the man said slowly while widening them as to emphasize his words. It wasn't the first time he had come across someone he thought was learning deficient and it really ticked him off that one of *them* would be stupid enough to try to steal his precious bike.

Understanding finally dawned on Heath as he said, "Oh. You mean the screen here sees your eyes and then turns it on."

"Duh," the man cleverly responded.

Heath quickly grabbed the man by the back of his head and slammed his face into the optical scan, hoping his eyes had remained open because he wasn't sure he would get a second chance. The cycle roared to life as Heath let go of the unconscious stranger.

"Sorry guy, but it's an emergency," Heath said without remorse and drove away.

Aphrodite kneeled in the cramped bubble. Even if there had been room to stand, terror kept her frozen in place. She stared out fearfully, wondering if the crazy ride would end soon. She wasn't sure how high up she was but it was definitely beyond the limits of her vision. She was near-sighted but refused to wear her glasses, especially at school. She knew the glasses would be one more reason to pile on with insults and she just didn't feel like hearing them. And unfortunately, her eyes were too sensitive for contact lenses and rejected them every time she had tried to put them in.

She had managed to get away with being visually impaired because most of the teachers sat the students in alphabetical order and her last name began with the second letter of the alphabet. When students were switched around due to classroom management or the teacher allowed the students to assign their own seat, she would rely on her strengths of being an auditory learner. But this situation was different and she regretted leaving her glasses in the past. She looked down hoping she could decipher the blur she was passing over. As she squinted, she could make out several neighborhoods below her as she passed over them but she didn't recognize the streets.

She felt a shift in the direction she was traveling in and when she looked ahead she saw she was merging with a convoy of numerous spheres containing garbage bags of varying colors and sizes, traveling slowly in the same direction as if they were commuting to work.

Looks like rush hour, she thought to herself.

As she continued to stare out the orb, she suddenly realized her breathing was becoming shallow. She tried not to gasp as she became aware of the fact she was running out of oxygen.

Heath zipped through the neighborhood, mesmerized by a corner house as he passed by it that had a hugger-mugger of colorful flowers occupying half of the front lawn as if the owners had planted every type of flower that existed as a shout out to *Better Homes and Gardens.* There were red, pink and yellow tulips, purple pansies, vibrant sunflowers and other brilliant blossoms he couldn't identify. It was obvious the owners with the not so green thumbs had been neglecting their garden because some of the flowers had begun to wilt, reminding Heath of a decomposing rainbow.

In his hurry to catch up to Aphrodite, Heath nearly ran over a rather surprised pedestrian who didn't seem to believe in looking both ways before crossing the street. A voice began to emanate from the motorcycle, repeatedly asking Heath if he wanted to switch to auto-drive. He didn't know what that meant and hoped the vehicle wouldn't make the decision for him. He looked down at the optical scan and saw that it now displayed an instrument panel, informing him of his speed and his power-cell needing to be recharged soon. Ignoring the invisible nag in the cycle, he eventually made it out of the burbs and within minutes, he was ascending the highway on-ramp. He weaved dangerously through traffic, trying unsuccessfully to catch up to the bubble that had imprisoned Aphrodite. The bubble suddenly veered off into a different direction that Heath would not be able to follow on his current course. He was going north and Aphrodite was now going west, along with a procession of several other globes, containing what looked like garbage bags.

"Crap!"

He was worried the wind would blow the stupid thing all over the city but he quickly realized that the few trees he could see from the highway, were as still as statues. There was no wind. For some reason, he thought that was worse. He needed to catch up and he needed to do it now. Without much thought and relying on instinct alone, Heath sped the bike up, crossed the median and found himself on the opposite side of the highway and into oncoming traffic. Heath was nearly hit several times but somehow managed to avoid any collisions as he continued to drive upstream. When he spotted the on-ramp to his left, he quickly swerved in that direction, managing to evade an onslaught of oncoming cars. When he finally reached the entrance of the on-ramp, Heath made a quick right, sped up and gratefully discovered he had successfully subtracted a good deal of miles between himself and Aphrodite's sphere.

For one brief moment, he allowed himself to bask in the bliss of riding on a speeding bike.

Aphrodite was gasping desperately for breath, unsure of when the next one would be her last. Though she usually felt that she was ready for death's cold embrace, she wanted it to be under her terms.

Not this way. Definitely not this way.

Just as she started to black out, the bubble burst, depositing her into a large, metal bin. Her sudden fall was thankfully broken by a massive pile of garbage bags that been dropped in before her. A bag hit her on the head while three more landed next to her as the last of the day's garbage made their way to their final resting place.

"Ow!" Aphrodite looked around her new prison and surmised that the rectangular box she fell into was similar to the ones from her time, just bigger. She looked up and saw that she wasn't too far away from the mouth of the green container. If she could just reach it, she would be able to pull herself out.

She heard the cracking and scraping of glass bottles as she tried to stand in the deep container but the trash bags made it impossible for her to find her footing. She accidentally ripped some of the flimsy bags with her shoes in her failed attempts to stand and her lower pant-legs were slowly being coated in rancid refuse.

"Aphrodite!" Hearing her name, she looked up

and saw Heath grinning down at her.

"It's not funny. Even in the future I'm treated like garbage."

"At least we're closer to the city," he said, trying to stifle his laughter.

"Great," she mumbled.

"Ten seconds to incineration," an invisible male voice announced.

Heath looked confused as he asked, "What does that mean?" But Aphrodite understood the voice's warning.

"It means get me out of here now!" she shouted.

Heath leaned his body over the lip of the container and reached out his hand to her. He wobbled a bit as his balance was at the mercy of the crates he had stacked to reach the top of the bin.

As Aphrodite stood clumsily and tried to maintain her precarious balance, they both heard the disembodied voice counting down, "Ten, nine, eight…" Their hands finally found each other as Heath's right hand gripped Aphrodite's, and wrapped itself like a python that had finally found its prey.

He quickly lifted her out and they both tumbled to the ground, followed by the stack of crates as the unseen voice continued, "…three, two, one." As they lay on the ground, a huge burst of light radiated from the bin, obliterating everything that had been inside.

Unable to take her eyes off the bin, Aphrodite

said tremulously, "Thanks."

"No problem," Heath replied, his voice uneven as he gawped at the box that nearly killed them both.

The smell of ionized air made Aphrodite's nose crinkle and she finally lost interest in the empty container. She looked over at Heath and laughed.

"Your hair is standing up," she chortled.

Heath touched his hands to his hair and felt his new awful hairstyle. He immediately tried to flatten it back down hoping he didn't look too silly.

"Your hair's the same," he observed which caused Aphrodite to glare at Heath.

Having both sobered up from the shock, they got to their feet. They brushed dirt off themselves, and then silently made their way to the city.

It was dark by the time they set foot in the city. Even with the faded light, they both could see the concrete landscape had changed over the years. Familiar buildings still stood where they had last seen them while others had been replaced by larger, more modern looking edifices. The metropolis bustled with traffic and people, who seemed to be oblivious to the two newcomers.

"Do you think anyone will notice we're…out of area?" Heath wondered aloud.

"Hope not or it might complicate things," she responded. Aphrodite had the same thought earlier but now that she had gotten a closer look at the inhabitants, she noted that fashion hadn't changed much in nearly three decades. It seemed they wouldn't stand out like a couple of sore tourists. "But I think we're good," she added.

Heath suddenly stopped walking and when Aphrodite realized she was several steps ahead of him, she stopped and turned to look at him.

"What?" she asked, her tone confused.

"We should probably find a place to sleep. I don't think we're getting anything done tonight," Heath suggested.

"I agree. We can start tomorrow but where are we going to go? We don't' have any money and we don't know anyone."

"There's got to be something," Heath insisted. They both ambled down the sidewalk, looking for anything that might make a decent, temporary abode. Heath stopped at an alleyway and gestured to it.

Aphrodite looked at him incredulously and said, "I am so not sleeping outside. Next..."

"We still have the house. We can always stay there," he proposed.

"Yeah, but I think it's too far from the city and I have a feeling that we should stick to this area. We'll lose too much time going back and forth," she explained wearily. She looked away and in that moment she spotted a homeless shelter employee just a few feet away, getting ready to close up for the night.

Wow. All this time and they still haven't solved this problem, she thought somberly to herself. Aphrodite sprinted towards the employee.

"Excuse me! Wait! Don't close the door yet!" she shouted to the bearded man at the doorway.

Heath easily kept up with her but had no idea what she had in mind.

The man, whose ID badge identified him as Henry, was surprised as he watched Heath and Aphrodite running towards him and stopped what he was doing. He closed the door behind him, suspicious of their intentions.

"How can I help you?" Henry asked when they finally reached him. Henry crossed his arms over his chest, half-covering the logo of his favorite college football team.

"We're new in town and we need a place to stay," Aphrodite told him, still a bit winded.

"Well there're plenty of hotels in the area," the man stated, eyeing them guardedly.

"We don't have any money," Heath said, trying to sound as pathetic as possible.

The man sighed in resignation. He really didn't have time to see if they were on the up and up and by the looks of their clothes it was obvious they weren't wearing the latest trend or designer name. He wasn't sure if they were wearing retro clothes which could be back in style for all he knew, or just really old but well-kept garments.

He tucked his hands into the front pockets of his jeans and finally said, “I have one bed left. One of you is more than welcome to stay in it.”

Heath and Aphrodite looked at each other perplexed. Neither one knew how they would decide which one would get to sleep semi-comfortably for the night.

Heath considered tossing a coin but didn’t have one on him and then wondered if they still existed in the future.

Aphrodite’s eyes narrowed as she studied Heath’s face. He appeared distracted enough that she might be able to shove him out of the way and just run in.

You snooze you lose, she cackled in her head.

But before she could make her move Heath said, “You take it. I’ll sleep in the alleyway.”

Feeling guilty, Aphrodite told him, “You can’t do that. That wouldn’t be fair.”

In a whisper so he wouldn’t be overheard, Heath suggested, “Then I’ll go to the house.”

As much as Aphrodite would like to get away from Heath for a few hours, separating might prove to be catastrophic.

“You shouldn’t be by yourself. Not here.” Aphrodite turned her attention to Henry and said, “Do you think he and I could stay in the same bed? We’re new in town and we're broke. I promise that there won't be any funny business. We don't even like each other."

Henry was still doubtful but her last statement was the most sincere thing he had heard her say.

"Then what are you two doing here?" he questioned.

"We have a job to do but we haven't found it yet," Heath answered honestly.

Understanding swept across the man's face as he said, "Oh. You're looking for employment."

"Yes. Exactly. And we have nowhere to stay. Please?" Aphrodite implored.

The man thought about all the poor souls inside the shelter that shared the young couple's predicament. All of them were waiting for someone to give them a chance. Through the years, many of the faces have remained the same while others disappeared only to be replaced by new ones. He still wasn't sure if he could trust the couple, but he couldn't help but think that he might be the only chance they would ever get. Besides, a few minutes ago, the girl gave her companion a look that appeared murderous. He decided the young man might live longer if the girl got some sleep.

Finally, Henry swung the front door open and said, "All right, but if anyone asks, I thought there were two beds."

Heath and Aphrodite spooned uncomfortably on the small cot. It was past midnight, but neither one could sleep and not just because they were adrift in a sea of snoring strangers who reeked of sweat and urine. Heath had a face full of Aphrodite's hair that pleasantly smelled like strawberries, which he hoped he wouldn't choke on while he slept. At least it countered the feted stench of body odor that surrounded them and Aphrodite's putrid pants.

Aphrodite had her own distraction.

"That better be the pen in your pocket," she said through gritted teeth.

"Don't flatter yourself," Heath scoffed.

The cot creaked in complaint as Aphrodite squirmed in a failed attempt to get less uncomfortable. Heath, whose arms were awkwardly wrapped around her, tightened his grip to stop her.

"Could you please stop squirming?" Heath said, emphasizing each word with an irritated tone.

"I can't help it. I'm not used to sleeping like this."

"What? With a hot guy?" he said mockingly.

Aphrodite considered head butting Heath with the back of her head. She had been listening to him spitting out her hair all night. Maybe if she gave him a mouthful of the stuff, she could shut him up until morning.

Instead, she explained, "No. I'm just used to

having more space."

Heath chuckled darkly and said, "Well, there's plenty of space on the floor if you need it that badly. By the way, roaches still exist in the future."

Aphrodite rolled her eyes and said, "I think I can deal with it, knowing the pen is the biggest thing in your pants."

Heath's smirk disappeared and shifted his body, forcing Aphrodite to fall off the bed. She landed on the floor with a dull thud.

"Whoops. I told you to stop squirming," he said coldly.

Aphrodite looked at Heath with venom, causing him to flinch. If looks could kill, there would be nothing left of him but a chalk outline on the thin mattress.

In a kneeling position, she shoved Heath to the farthest edge of the bed and climbed back in, causing the small metal frame to creak. She elbowed him in the stomach as hard as she could.

"Oops," she said insincerely as Heath gasped for breath. Wincing in pain, Heath forcefully wrapped his arms around her once again as they reluctantly spooned, grudgingly enjoying the smell of her hair. It was going to be a long night.

The next morning, Heath and Aphrodite got up early and quietly strolled through the city, looking for anything that seemed like a good place for them to start.

So far, just about every building they walked past was a bank, an office building or a store. They had been walking for an hour but nothing caught their attention. Heath was the first to break the silent tension between the two of them.

"Do you think they've realized we're missing?" he asked.

"I'm sure they've noticed you've disappeared. I bet half the city is out looking for you," replied Aphrodite, refusing to look at him.

Heath found her answer a bit odd.

"What about your parents?" he prodded further.

"They're probably looking for you too," she said dryly.

Heath couldn't tell if she was being serious. There was something in her voice that gave the impression she wanted to drop the subject. That wasn't about to happen.

"Don't you think they're worried about you?" he continued.

"Not really. They're probably happy I finally did something that didn't involve brooding." After a moment she added, "Relax. When you went into the future at the Bailey House, you were only gone for a few seconds. Your family will probably never know you were missing." He let out a small sigh of relief, but his thoughts focused on something Aphrodite had said earlier.

"You really think nobody cares about you?" he asked amusedly.

"Has anyone ever given me a reason to believe otherwise? Which reminds me, why did you guys start picking on me to begin with?"

Heath contemplated her inquiry for a moment. He honestly couldn't remember. It had started so many years ago and even then he wasn't sure they had a definitive reason to choose her as their initial target. They just did.

"I don't know," he finally said. "Your name maybe?"

Aphrodite stopped walking as her head swiveled quickly and finally looked at him. Her eyes were narrowed and her mouth resembled a snarl. He could feel the heat of hatred emanating from her stare.

"Do you mean to tell me, I have been your verbal punching bag for five years and you're not sure why?" she bellowed angrily.

"Well, you're also kind of ugly," he added in a low voice.

"You're unbelievable!" she shouted at him. For the first time in five years, Heath came face to face with the fruits of his cruelty.

"I'm sorry," he said feebly.

"You're sorry? My self-esteem has been shredded into confetti which you guys threw in my face over and over again and I've struggled for years to find reasons to like myself so that at least one person in this world does, but you're sorry? Screw you!"

Aphrodite quickly played back in her mind, the numerous verbal assaults aimed at her by Heath and his friends from over the years, feeling like their words were once again chiseling away at her worth. But now she couldn't decide what was more hurtful, the words themselves or the fact that she may have been a random target all this time.

It could have been anyone but they chose me for some sick reason, she thought. She imagined the phantom being who could have been her all these years and pitied them. As much as it sucked to be her, she didn't wish her pain on anyone else.

Seeing Aphrodite without her iron mask, Heath felt guilty. He and his friends never stuck around long enough to see the desolation from their destruction.

"But we never saw you cry," he said defensively.

Aphrodite looked at him incredulously and said sarcastically, "Oh, I'm sorry I never rewarded your efforts with my tears." She finally turned away from him and angrily stalked away.

Heath kept up with her enraged pace as she continued her tirade.

"I want you to know that when this is done, so are we. When we get back to our time, I don't want you to talk to me, look at me or stand within a hundred feet of me. I don't care if you find a calculator that opens a vortex in your ass!"

Heath slowed his pace, creating some distance between the two of them.

Aphrodite didn't get too far when a street cop stopped her.

"Can I help you and your friend?" he asked deferentially. "You seem upset and really loud."

Heath had overheard the policeman as he walked over to them. He became worried that they had drawn some unwanted attention, which was something they could not afford. For once, Aphrodite was speechless so Heath improvised a lie.

"It's okay, officer," Heath said as soon as he reached the two of them. "She's lost her dog and she's really worried," he added as believably as possible.

The officer relaxed slightly. He had two dogs of his own which he loved as much as his children and sympathized with the distraught girl.

"What about his pinger?" he asked in a sensitive tone.

Heath and Aphrodite looked at each other confused, each one hoping that the other understood what the policeman was talking about.

"Uh...we had him fixed recently and I don't think it works like it used to," Aphrodite explained, hoping she was giving the right answer. But as soon as the words were out of her mouth, the officer's brows furrowed and she knew she had screwed up.

"Let me try this again," his voice tinged with annoyance. "Have you tried pinging his chip?" he asked slowly, as if they were a couple of five-year-olds who still didn't know their own names.

Again, Heath and Aphrodite looked at each other. Heath shrugged his shoulders signaling Aphrodite to supply an answer again.

She finally looked back at the cop and said meekly, "It's broken?"

The cop sighed deeply. The tension had left his face so Aphrodite assumed that she had finally provided a reasonable response.

"What type of dog is he? Maybe I've seen him."

But before Aphrodite could answer, Heath spoke. "It's an Irish…horn-dog."

The officer's face which had been yo-yoing between annoyance and sympathy, returned to its irritated state.

"Funny. Get out of here before I bring you in for public stupidity."

Mortified, Heath and Aphrodite walked away from the cop, both hoping he wouldn't change his mind.

When they were far enough from him, Aphrodite hissed, "An Irish horn dog? That's not a breed you moron, that's you." She stormed away angrily yet relieved that things had not gone worse.

Heath found Aphrodite's severe mood swings annoying. He was beginning to think she had multiple personalities and all of them were pissing him off. He continued to shadow her from a remote distance wondering if they would save the future before they killed each other.

Heath's feet ached from walking on the hard pavement. His legs were becoming heavier with each step as if the cement was draining the strength from his limbs. Aside from the lack of sleep from the night before, he was tired of walking and being ignored by Aphrodite. Yet he was impressed that she kept a consistent swift pace, only slowing down when something caught her eye. She seemed to be scrutinizing each building they passed by, but as soon as she felt they were useless, she would pick up her pace again.

"What are you looking for?" Heath called out to her. He was surprised when she answered him.

"The library," she replied coldly. After a few more steps she added, "I just don't understand why we haven't found it."

Heath clearly wasn't familiar with the Broward County Main Library. Had he been, he would have known that it was located on South Andrews Avenue, which they had passed an hour ago. Despite all the trees that crowded its front lawn, the eight-story building was hard to miss. Aphrodite always thought the library resembled a set of glass steps that seemed to lead to nowhere. Before she had made the Bailey attic her fortress of solitude, she used to spend hours in the library and became familiar with most of its contents which she had hoped would lead them to some answers. Now, more to her dismay than surprise, there was a condominium in its place and it didn't seem they had moved the library to a new location.

"Maybe they don't have one," Heath supposed.

"Don't be stupid," she chided him. "Every city has a library. Why doesn't this one?" she said flailing her arms with frustration.

Heath understood the future less than she did and thought that perhaps they should change their approach.

"Maybe we should try something else," he proposed, hoping it would lead to a reprieve from the excess exercise and heat. Aphrodite stopped suddenly and quickly turned to face Heath who froze in mid-step.

"Okay. What do you suggest?" she asked dryly.

"I don't know. I just want this to be over with so I don't have to suffer through another terrible night."

"Don't worry. I'm not going to let that happen," she told him confidently.

We're not really in the future. We're in hell, Heath thought to himself as he lay awkwardly on the small cot with his arms wrapped around Aphrodite, the strawberry scent slightly faded from her hair. It was going to be another sleepless night. He could tell she was awake as well, because her body had remained tense from the second they both climbed into the miniscule bed. He recalled their fight from earlier that day and became curious.

"How did you get your name anyway," he asked, hoping it wouldn't instigate a new argument. Aphrodite remained silent and Heath assumed she still didn't want to talk to him.

"My parents are Greek mythology freaks," she answered quietly. "I guess it didn't occur to them that I would never live up to the name. But it could have been worse. If I had been a boy, my name would have been Hephaestus." She sighed deeply as she thought about the unfortunate looking god who was also familiar with rejection. "I look like a Hephaestus."

Heath felt Aphrodite's body become less tense as it deflated from depression.

"Don't feel so bad. I was named for a candy bar," he said.

"You're kidding!" she said with a mix of surprise and amusement.

"Yeah, I am," he admitted sheepishly. Aphrodite smiled to herself and then shared with Heath what she had been thinking for days.

"Do you ever wonder about the pen?"

"What do you mean?"

"Like, who made it? Is it alien technology? And if it is, why did they make it and leave it here on Earth? Or even better, what if it's some sort of divine tool?" She sighed, lost in her bewilderment. She couldn't help wondering about its origins and the possibility of others coming into contact with it as well. The stories they could tell.

"Hello...It's a pen," Heath said as he tapped her on the head with it.

"Yes, thank you Heath," she responded sardonically.

They lay quietly in the dark for a few moments when Heath finally asked, "Are you still mad at me?"

"You'll know if you wake up tomorrow," she answered tersely.

Aphrodite closed her eyes hoping sleep would finally stop by to visit her while Heath remained wide awake.

Three days later, Heath and Aphrodite were repeating the same routine they had established since they had arrived in the future. The only difference was that frustration had kicked anxiety to the curb.

Heath suddenly stopped where he stood and held up his hands as if he surrendered.

"We've been here almost a week and all we've done is sleep, and walk around the city four times. We've become friggin tourists," Heath complained.

Aphrodite didn't want to argue with him because she was too tired but more than anything, he was right.

"I know. The shelter food doesn't help either but

I don't know where to start looking." They had taken a gamble. Perhaps it was time to admit they would have to go home without any chips. "Maybe we should go back to our time and start all over again," she said, feeling defeated. Her words sobered up Heath. He wasn't ready to quit yet.

"We're already here. We're just missing something," he said, trying to convince himself as well. Aphrodite looked away thoughtfully, biting her bottom lip. When she looked back at Heath, he watched as her lip quickly regained its pinkish hue.

"Maybe it's time for us to do something drastic," she said in a somber tone. They only had one more option and she wasn't sure how he would react to it.

Heath's hairs stood on end as he asked, "How drastic?"

She looked him in the eyes hesitantly.

"Make contact with ourselves in the future," she said in a near whisper. Heath's anxious face mirrored what Aphrodite was feeling and he began to pace.

"I thought that was supposed to be a bad idea."

Aphrodite's eyes followed his muddled path.

"It is but I just don't see any other alternative. Even if we find a library, or whatever, we still don't know what we're looking for." Her words brought him no comfort but he was willing to admit that they had hit a wall. He stopped pacing and met her eyes with his.

"Okay. Who do you want to look for?"

"At this point, whoever we can find," she answered.

They walked a few feet and reached the corner end of the block where they found a glass communication booth. The small booth couldn't accommodate the two of them so Aphrodite stepped through the narrow opening while Heath leaned into it. It reminded Heath of the phone booths in the Superman comic books he used to read before he hit puberty. Standing outside of one, he didn't feel like much of a hero.

Aphrodite wasn't too sure how to use the device. She put her right hand to the holographic screen and a small image of slight middle-aged man, dressed in a charcoal suit replaced the screen. Heath and Aphrodite exchanged looks.

"How can I assist you?" the male avatar asked in a smooth polite voice.

"Uh…We need an address," Aphrodite stated meekly.

"Name please," commanded the avatar.

"Our name or the people we're looking for?" Heath asked Aphrodite with confusion.

"We're looking for ourselves," she reminded him, slightly vexed. She rolled her eyes and returned her attention to the small holographic man.

"Heath Wells," she stated slowly and clearly.

“Searching,” the avatar announced. The avatar’s face appeared to glaze over as seconds ticked by. He seemed to come back to life when he announced, “No such listing.”

Aphrodite looked to Heath who was more surprised than she was.

“I guess I moved away. I wonder where I live now?” he said, mostly to himself. Aphrodite was feeling anxious. They finally had a plan and they were zero for one. Not good.

Please be here, she thought to herself, worried that her future self never returned to Florida after finishing college.

“Aphrodite Buonarroti,” she said, annunciating her name as clearly as possible, hoping that it would increase their chances of finding her.

“Searching,” said the avatar. Aphrodite nervously ran her right hand through her hair, where it briefly got stuck on a huge knot.

The avatar suddenly disappeared and an address appeared on the screen.

“We got a hit,” Aphrodite said happily as she committed the address to memory. “Let’s go.”

9
Timeless

Heath and Aphrodite walked through the hallway of the condominium complex, where the address they were given was located. They stopped in front of a white doorway that supposedly belonged to the future Aphrodite. They glanced down both sides of the surprisingly plain hallway, making sure they had privacy. The off-white corridor really didn't match their expectations after seeing the lobby of the waterfront property which had been adorned with cherry wood paneling, two wall fountains made of dark stones beneath each side of a curved double stairwell, and an elaborate mosaic at the center of the marbled floor.

It was obvious that the building they were standing in was for a social class neither of them belonged to and they were surprised how easily they were given access to the upper floors. All they had to do was provide a thumbprint at the elevators and the silver doors opened as if they were residents returning home. Aphrodite was slightly impressed with her future self and raised her hand as she prepared to knock on the door. Heath spasmed with panic and stopped her.

"Are you just going to knock? Don't you think this will be hard on your future self?" Aphrodite pulled back her hand, realizing that it could be catastrophic if she followed through.

"You're right," she said to Heath. "Maybe if I disguise myself, I can slowly ease my future self into this." She gripped the rounded neckline of her dark t-shirt and pulled it up over her nose so that it covered the lower half of her face. "How do I look?" she asked, her voice muffled by the cotton material.

"Like you're about to rob your future self," Heath answered dubiously.

Aphrodite shook her head dismissively and then pushed him away from the doorway.

"You can't be standing there when future me opens the door. I might still remember you from high school and I don't think I can handle seeing both of us."

Heath found this slightly amusing and almost suggested she should always wear her shirts half way up her face but then thought better of it. Instead, he followed her orders but made sure he was still close enough to listen.

Aphrodite gave Heath once last glance before knocking on the door. To her surprise, the door slid open and a stranger was on the other side of it. Aphrodite stared at the young woman, dumbfounded. The girl had short dark hair, green eyes and was probably just a few years older than Aphrodite. Her beige slacks and tucked-in yellow blouse made it even more obvious Aphrodite was not looking at her future self.

"Can I help you?" the young woman asked, her tone and expression puzzled by the stranger who seemed to be experiencing a wardrobe malfunction. Aphrodite suddenly felt foolish wearing her shirt over her face and quickly pulled it down.

"Oh, sorry. I must have the wrong apartment," she said apologetically.

But the young woman's eyes widened as if she were stunned, rolled into the back of her head and she suddenly fell to the floor. Heath, hearing the commotion, popped his head through the open doorway and peered at the unconscious woman.

"Why did you hit her?" he asked.

"I didn't. She looked at me and fainted," she said defensively.

Heath understood the strange woman's reaction and said, "Well…"

"Don't you dare finish that sentence," Aphrodite said threateningly. "Help me move her," she commanded Heath.

They both bent over the woman and lifted her. They shuffled their way to a large, brown leather sofa and placed her body down as gently as possible.

Heath ran back to the doorway and found the button that controlled the door. Oddly enough, it looked like a doorbell. He pressed the button and the door slid closed with a soft hiss. He ran back to the sofa where Aphrodite was sitting, lightly slapping the woman on the face. "Lady! Lady, wake up! Lady!"

Heath sat at the woman's feet and studied her

face which was slowly developing a hand- print shaped blush. The woman had an attractive face and resembled Aphrodite yet she looked slightly different. He couldn't help thinking that she had some facial features that reminded Heath of someone else but just couldn't put his finger on who it was.

Maybe she had some work done, he thought to himself. Whatever it was, she no longer looked like the Aphrodite he was travelling with.

"You look pretty good in the future," he remarked.

"That's because it's not me," she responded through gritted teeth.

"Then who is she?"

The woman's eyes suddenly flitted open. She quickly sat up, looked at Aphrodite and threw her arms around her, hugging her closely.

"Mom!" she sobbed, as her grip seemed to get tighter and tighter. "I've missed you!" The young woman sobbed as she embraced Aphrodite, who looked to Heath, for some sign that it was a practical joke he had somehow engineered.

A huge grin appeared on Heath's face and he began to laugh.

"What?" she asked angrily.

"I thought for sure you'd die a virgin," he replied, still amused.

The strange woman finally released Aphrodite,

turned to look at Heath as if she suddenly realized he was in the room and lunged at him, hugging him tightly.

"Dad!"

"What?" Heath and Aphrodite shouted at the same time. Heath's face was overcome with panic.

"Are you sure you didn't hit her?" he demanded.

The woman let go of Heath, wiped away her tears as she looked at them and said, "I'm your daughter, Jane." Tears continued to rain down her face but she was no longer crying.

Aphrodite felt bile rise in her throat as she said, "No. No. If you're our daughter, then that would mean he and I…" she gestured between herself and Heath "…yuck." Aphrodite went from panic to full fledge nuclear melt-down, trying to figure out how such a horrible thing could come to pass. She jumped out of her seat and paced the room saying, "Oh, my God! Oh, my God! I'm a drug addict in the future!"

Jane's brows knitted together and said, "I don't think you ever did drugs, Mom."

Aphrodite stopped walking, turned to face Jane and said, "Could you please stop calling me that."

But Jane only smiled at her, rose from the sofa and went over to hug Aphrodite again.

"I can't help it. I've missed you guys so much." Jane finally ended the hug, pushing away from her, but still holding on so she could face Aphrodite. Jane's face was a collage of emotions as she said, "How are you here? I don't care. But you're so young. It doesn't matter. You're here." She hugged Aphrodite, who was too overwhelmed to speak.

Heath, who had finally overcome his shock, was curious.

"You keep saying you've missed us. Do we not visit you enough?"

Jane broke off her hug with Aphrodite to look at him.

"No. But I visit you all the time," she said in a tone that matched her sober face.

Heath, Aphrodite and Jane stood in a cemetery just outside the city. Gone were the traditional grassy plots and gray headstones. They had been replaced with metal posts that individually projected various Sepia toned images of children at play, smiling adults and elderly faces who would age no more. From a distance, the cemetery looked like it was being invaded by a swarm of giant reddish-brown lightening bugs.

The three of them were gathered around a round post, etched with Heath and Aphrodite's names, which projected a holographic slideshow of their life together just above it. The incandescent faces, who were obviously no longer teenagers, were shown in various stages of their lives such as them beaming as they held a new-born baby and briefly kissing after Aphrodite blew out two candles shaped like a four and a zero perched on a birthday cake. Several other images flashed by, but Heath had turned away unable to watch himself aging and developing creases around his eyes and mouth. Having already confronted his mortality with the motorcycle accident and attending the funerals of some of his more ancient relatives whose time had come, standing where he stood had become overwhelming. Jane saw his face and could see her father was struggling with the knowledge of his exact date of death.

"There was a car accident a few years ago," Jane said, her voice quivering as she tried not to cry. Heath was having a difficult time processing her words.

"But it's the future. Everything is supposed to be better in the future."

"I wish that was true," Jane said, putting her hand on Heath's arm, rubbing it softly.

"So we're not here?" Aphrodite asked dazed.

Jane shook her head, unable to verbally confirm their tragic demise.

Seeing the shock on Aphrodite's face, Heath leaned into her ear and whispered, "Isn't that what you wanted?" She shot him an angry look but was too stunned to answer him. Knowing when she finally met her end, with Heath no less, left her at a loss for words and coherent thought. According to the holo-grave, they would be dead in twenty-four years.

"Not that I want to further ruin our family

reunion but do you think you guys could explain a few things to me?" Jane asked.

10
Lifetime

Jane sat on her sofa, mouth agape, holding the pen in the hand, which had finally stopped trembling. She was desperately trying to process the words coming from the two teens sitting across from her.

"So, you're from the past? Two-thousand fourteen?" she asked incredulously.

Aphrodite, who sat on the far side of the sofa from her said, "Yes." And quietly wished the sofa had been longer.

"And you two aren't dating?" she asked, looking first to Aphrodite and then to Heath who was standing, too anxious to sit.

"Please. We're not even friending," Aphrodite scoffed.

A brief look of disappointment rolled across Jane's face and then it returned to astonishment.

"And something really bad is going to happen but you don't know what it is?"

"Exactly," Heath answered. Jane seemed to be going down a mental checklist, having them reconfirm everything they had just told her.

"And this is a time machine?" she asked holding out the pen.

"Yes," they both answered at once.

Jane looked away thoughtfully and said, "No

wonder you got mad at me."

"What are you talking about?" Aphrodite asked.

"I came across this pen when I was five and you two flipped out and grounded me for a year. You told Dad to hide it after that." Heath and Aphrodite looked at each other, both of them surprised.

"We kept the pen," he said to her, his voice tinged with awe.

"And now you need my help," Jane said, regaining their attention.

"We wouldn't have bothered you but I don't think this is something we can figure out by ourselves no matter how many times we come back to this time. We need someone who understands the future," Aphrodite said earnestly.

Jane didn't even need a moment to think.

"Tell me what you need from me," she said insistently.

"We need access to information. Maybe there's something that will clue us in," Aphrodite told her.

"We tried looking for a library but we couldn't find one," Heath explained.

Jane chuckled to herself as if an inside joke between friends had been spoken.

"That's because they became obsolete years ago. Everyone has access to all kinds of information right at home," she said, leading them to her dining room. At first, Aphrodite admired the beautiful rectangular dining room table with a merlot finish and its curved trestle base but then she realized Jane didn't take them there to show off her furniture. In the far corner was a small table with a dusty desk top computer and a large flat-screen monitor.

"A computer," Aphrodite said with satisfaction. She was happy to see something she finally recognized. "Now we're talking."

"Don't be silly," Jane laughed. We only kept that dinosaur around as a conversation piece. This is what we use now," she said pointing, and returned Aphrodite's attention back to the dining table.

She noticed the small metal wafer which lay in the center of the long table. Jane waved her hand over it and a large holographic screen appeared.

"No more books?" Heath asked, impressed. He thought that maybe the digital books that became popular during his time may have driven them to extinction.

"Not like the ones you're familiar with. Whatever you want can be called up with this," she explained holding up what appeared to be a large, hardcover book that had no title or author. She opened the book to show them it also lacked words. It was a collection of blank pages. "Pride and Prejudice," Jane said aloud. She opened the book once more as if she were a teacher about to read from a picture book to her class. Words suddenly began to appear on the pages, and Heath and

Aphrodite assumed it was the story Jane had dictated.

"They developed this when people complained that reading off the vid or using a digital book was bothering their eyes. They've done the same thing with magazines." She placed the book on a counter and picked up what looked like a naked periodical.

"So people still read in the future?" Heath asked, disappointed. Jane smiled at him.

"Well, you can have D.A.T.A. read to you as well, but yes, people still read books in the future," she said with amusement.

"Data?" Aphrodite repeated.

"It stands for Digitally Advanced Transceiving Apparatus. The word computer just didn't cover it anymore," Jane explained.

"So you can call up anything you want and it will appear in the book?" Aphrodite asked.

"Or the D.A.T.A. Only a few people have issues with reading digital media. Others just missed turning pages," Jane clarified. She put the blank magazine down on the counter, next to the D.A.T.A. book and said, "So tell me. What are your theories?"

Heath shrugged his shoulders and said, "I don't know. War?"

Jane smiled dourly as she recalled the global conflicts over the last few years. The battles involved many of the same countries whose sole purpose of existence seemed to be initiating warfare. But for Jane, even the good guys could easily be confused with the bad.

"Technology made things uglier before they got better. But it's not an issue anymore," she said.

"What happened?" Heath asked.

"Some years ago, the arms race became a global game of nuclear chicken with the winner starting Armageddon. But certain leaders were outnumbered by people who enjoyed living so they were jailed, overthrown, or assassinated. Even our country went through a change as well," Jane stated. A shiver went up her spine as she recalled the countless times the world came close to a third and final major war.

Aphrodite found this information intriguing. Maybe there was more to this than Jane realized.

"What kind of change?" Aphrodite asked, hoping for more details.

"We finally elected a third party into office. Thank God, too, because we were quickly becoming a police state." Jane shuddered, remembering how living in a free country had suddenly come with a huge price. New restrictive laws kept getting passed while the voters continued to alternate between the two major political parties during the elections, only to get the same rotten results. Eventually, a group of Libertarians broke off from their own party to form a new one- The Plebeian Party, which the current president of the United States was a member of. She had begun to slowly undo the damage with the help of her peers in Congress. Citizens no longer worried about tapped phones, buzzing drones, or laws that were meant to diminish their rights.

"Like Big Brother?" Aphrodite asked.

Jane smiled affectionately at her and replied, "You used to call it Little Sister because the system wasn't good for anything except getting you in trouble."

Jane looked to both of them, a ghost of her previous smile remained on her face. Though she had been deeply involved in their conversation, a small part of her mind was having thoughts of its own.

She stood up and announced, "We need a break. When was the last time you two showered?"

"That would be two-thousand fourteen," Aphrodite answered drolly.

Jane held out her hand to her mother and said, "Come with me, Mom. Dad, there's a shower you can use down the hallway, first door on the right."

Aphrodite stood up, looked back at Heath apprehensively and then allowed herself to be led by Jane to her master bedroom.

Jane stood in her walk-in closet, scrounging around for clothes, as blouses fell to the floor from their perches. The closet floor was littered with several expensive dresses and shirts that had fallen victim to her scavenging. She stepped on them carelessly as she moved around the large storage space, searching for the perfect top.

Aphrodite stood by the dresser, scrutinizing picture frames that flashed a montage of photos of herself, Heath and Jane and several unfamiliar faces, as it cycled their images over various years.

A thought occurred to Aphrodite and asked loudly, “Why is the apartment under my name?”

Jane popped her head out of the closet and answered sheepishly, “Oh, I was using your name as a stage name. Jane Wells is so dull but yours is so colorful and beautiful.”

Aphrodite blushed slightly, never having heard her name described that way.

“So you’re an actress?”

Jane emerged from the closet, holding a pink, fitted polo shirt and khaki pants.

“No. I only did it for a while. Turned out no matter what my name was, I wasn’t a very good actress,” she said, laughing at herself. She handed the folded clothes to Aphrodite and said, “Here. We’re about the same size so this should fit you.”

Aphrodite took the clothes from her.

“Thanks,” she said appreciatively, and realized that she had never wanted a shower and a change of clothes so much in her life.

Aphrodite sat self-consciously at the vanity in Jane’s expansive bathroom. She and Jane might share the same genes, but they definitely had different tastes. Though Jane had been right and the outfit she now wore fit her perfectly, she would rather still be wearing her ill-fitting, stench ridden shirt and pants. She felt safe in her own clothes. But wearing Jane's pink V-neck shirt and khaki pants, she felt like a mutt at the Westminster Dog Show. She wasn't exactly overweight but she didn't have a cheerleader's body, with perfectly toned arms and abs. She wore a B-cup, which looked more like an A minus underneath her extra-large shirts so she was slightly surprised when the pink shirt that clinged to her torso, reminded her that she actually had cleavage. Staring at her image, which was reflected back to her but not through a mirror, she felt the dog metaphor was appropriate. Even though she had washed it, her untamable hair, nearly dried, seemed wilder than usual and her face had sprouted several more pimples since arriving in the future. She hated seeing herself. The way she avoided mirrors, she was like a vampire trying not to give herself away. But Jane had told her to sit there and wait for her.

Jane finally walked into the bathroom and saw the reflected image of Aphrodite's glum face. She knew what her mother was thinking and was determined to change her mind.

"I need you to trust me," she said with a soft smile.

"This can't end well," Aphrodite said under her

breath. Jane removed what looked like a plastic facemask from one of the drawers in the vanity.

Before Aphrodite could ask what it was, Jane placed it over her face and it emitted a small cloud of steam. The hot vapor had a scent Aphrodite couldn't quite place but she was certain it smelled like medicine. Jane removed the mask and slowly wiped Aphrodite's face with a towel. When Aphrodite was able to look at her image again, she saw that not a single blemish remained on her face. Even the scars from previous pimples had become less visible.

Then Aphrodite did something she hadn't done since she was a child. She admired her reflection. She wasn't beautiful exactly but now that she was willing to look at herself for more than five seconds, she thought her heart shaped face, upturned nose and large almond eyes were not conspiring against her.

Jane, smiling broadly, interrupted her reverie when she explained, "You bought this as soon as it came out. You said we would thank you forever and, well, we do." Jane picked up a large square hair brush from the counter and appeared to be preparing to brush Aphrodite's hair.

Just as the silver bristles were going to make contact with her, Aphrodite waved her off and said, "Oh, don't even bother. It just makes it worse." Her hair had been quite beautiful when she was younger; thick waves that flowed down her back. But when puberty hit, her hair became course and the Florida humidity made it extra unmanageable. She eventually discovered that her maternal great-grandmother had similar hair and Aphrodite came to resent the unfortunate genetic hand-me-down. She had considered chopping it off several times but puberty had not only gifted her with bad hair but severe acne as well and her thick mane became an ideal veil. For now, she was content to have won one battle. If her hair were to fall out tomorrow, it would be an improvement and a relief.

But being a typical daughter, Jane ignored her mother and began to stroke Aphrodite's hair. To Aphrodite's shock, the brush left trails of smooth tresses in its wake.

"Wow," Aphrodite whispered with awe. "How did you do that?"

Jane's grin grew bigger and said, "Nano technology." She hoped Aphrodite wouldn't ask her to elaborate since she really didn't understand the technology herself. "If you use these products once a month, the changes become long-term." Aphrodite studied Jane's serene face through the reflection as she continued to brush her hair. Jane seemed to be lost in contentment, which Aphrodite found slightly disconcerting.

"You know, for someone whose dead parents suddenly showed up from the past while still teenagers, you seem to be handling it well."

Jane stopped brushing for a moment, processed the comment and decided how to respond to it. Miserable memories tugged down at her mouth as she recalled her loss.

"I'm sure you must think I'm crazy for not freaking out but I've missed you guys so much. You could have been flesh eating zombies and I still would have been happy to see you," Jane said with a smile.

"I guess we were a close family," Aphrodite pondered aloud.

"We were. We *all* were."

Jane's last comment triggered a realization for Aphrodite, as she recalled the strangers from the photos. One that stood out had been a dark haired girl that had long wavy hair. The strange girl with the dark eyes could have easily passed for Aphrodite's sister; or daughter. The other face that repeated several times as well had been a handsome boy with light brown hair and dimples that creased his face as he smiled. His hazel eyes reminded her of her own mother.

"Do you mean there are more of you?"

"I am the oldest of three. Mary and Apollo moved away after you died. They couldn't deal with the memories." Aphrodite gagged on air.

"Apollo?" she repeated.

"Grandma guilted you into that one," Jane explained. Jane remembered how her mother had fought tooth and nail against their grandmother when it came to the name. But on the day her brother was born, her parents took one look at his beautiful face and his name couldn't be anything but Apollo.

"Oh, please tell me he doesn't hate me for giving him that name," Aphrodite moaned. She couldn't understand why she dreaded the resentment of someone she had never met, but Aphrodite did anyway.

Jane smiled at her mother reassuringly and said, "He loves his name and he's always loved you." Jane finished brushing Aphrodite's hair and it draped down her shoulders like fine silk. She placed her hands on Aphrodite's shoulders and said, "You're beginning to look like the mom I remember."

Aphrodite's reflection smiled back at Jane, truly grateful for her transformation. Jane studied her mother's face briefly, absorbing every feature as if recommitting them to memory.

"Now go sit with Dad. We have a lot of talking to do," Jane said suddenly and forcefully. Startled by the change in her tone, Aphrodite stood up quickly but as she walked away Jane shouted, "Wait!"

Aphrodite stopped where she stood. Jane ran up to her and spritzed her with perfume.

"What was that?" Aphrodite asked.

Jane smiled mischievously and said, "Dad's favorite perfume. Now go."

Heath sat alone in the living room, wearing the change of clothes Jane had given him. His new jeans were a little loose at the waist and a few inches too long but the blue t-shirt she had given him fit perfectly. His right leg bounced nervously as if it had somewhere else to be and was running late. He couldn't believe he was stuck in the future with someone he knew but hated and someone he didn't know at all, yet had supposedly fathered.

He kept thinking about his real family and how much he missed them at the moment. His parents, who had supported him unconditionally, especially after the accident, were foremost in his thoughts. Despite what Aphrodite had told him, he wondered if they were worried about him and wished he had left them a note. It made him sick when he thought they might be trying to find him but would never succeed. He also thought about his younger brother Henry, who, despite only being in middle school, had the potential to be a star-quarterback. Though Heath had been jealous of him since the accident, he would now give anything to be in his backyard, playing catch with his only sibling. He reassured himself that everything would be fine when he returned to his time and it would be as if he never left.

He looked around the living room, taking in the warm colored walls and dark leather furniture. A pair of paintings depicting forest landscapes adorned the walls. Despite being in a stranger's residence, the contemporary space had a homey feel to it.

I wouldn't mind a room like this, someday, he thought to himself.

A silhouette walking down the unlit hallway towards the living room caught his attention. At first he thought it was Jane but the hair was too long. As the person came closer into the light, he realized how wrong he was. His mouth was agape as Aphrodite, who to his amazement, actually had a waistline, made her way to the sofa and sat next to him. But instead of sitting back and getting comfortable, she rested her elbows on her thighs and cupped her face, unaware of his gaze. He thought she no longer looked like an escaped mental patient with her long, smooth hair draping down the pink shirt she was wearing. Someone had finally slain that dragon.

Holy crap, she's wearing pink.

He leaned over trying to peek at her profile. He could also see that her face no longer had any blemishes. All they needed was Tiny Tim and a few ghosts and it would be a Christmas miracle. Except it was August. He slightly leaned into her and detected an appealing aroma and sniffed her quietly. She smelled of Jasmine, his favorite scent. Heath jumped in his seat when Aphrodite finally spoke.

"Did you know we had two more?"

"Two more what?" he asked with confusion.

"Kids! Mary and Apollo," she said, sounding

upset. He was taken aback by her strong, negative reaction to having a family.

"I thought all women wanted to have kids. You know, that biological clock thing." Aphrodite scoffed.

"Do you want to know what a biological clock is? It's the equivalent of some idiot being tricked into opening a hell dimension and releasing demons into the world," she explained, clearly upset. "Look at my minions. Don't they look just like me?" she added in a mocking tone.

Heath wasn't sure what a minion was but he still found her ranting humorous.

Jane walked into the room and scanned Heath quickly.

"I wasn't sure the clothes would fit but they seem perfect," she said sounding satisfied.

"Yeah, thanks," he replied.

Jane was thrilled to have her parents again but she found it unnatural how uncomfortable they looked with each other.

"I prepared the guest room," she said to them.

Heath and Aphrodite stared at each other, not sure which one she was speaking to.

"I'll take the sofa," Heath said finally.

"Oh. Yeah. You're not married. I'll bring you a pillow and blanket," she said disappointedly to Heath. "Come on Mom. I'll take you to your room."

Aphrodite couldn't sleep. She finally had a full size bed all to herself but she had been tossing and turning for almost an hour and a half. She pulled the taupe duvet cover up to her chin in frustration, feeling the goose feathers shift inside it, but she still found no peace. Despite having a soft mattress beneath her, her mind was crowded with several thoughts, clamoring for attention. She was overwhelmed thinking about what she had discovered about her future- being married to Heath, having a family, and being dead. She was also restless from what she didn't know about the future- what had they come to prevent? But what plagued her most was how alone she felt. After much deliberation, she got up from the bed and walked to the living room. She found Heath lying shirtless on the sofa, wide awake.

"Heath. Are you asleep?" she whispered.

"Yes," he hissed, clearly irritated that he wasn't.

"Will you sleep with me tonight?" she asked, not having put much thought into the question before she asked it.

"Excuse me?" Heath stammered and sat up. Mortified, he covered himself up with the fleece blanket Jane had provided him. Aphrodite was already irritated from insomnia and now she felt incensed that he would even think she was attracted to him.

"I didn't mean it that way. I just need someone to lie next to me. I'm kind of freaking out being in the future knowing we're here because we need to save the world and we're in an apartment with some girl who says she's our future daughter," she said in one breath.

Resigned, Heath's lips vibrated as he blew air through them, sounding like a frustrated horse.

"Fine. Whatever."

Heath and Aphrodite each lay on opposite sides of the guest bed, their eyes too troubled to close. They had been like that for nearly forty-five minutes. Heath, who had put on a shirt before climbing into bed with Aphrodite, had known for hours why sleep had eluded him. He sighed deeply, rolled over until he was close enough to Aphrodite and wrapped his arms around her. He had expected her to tense up and elbow him in the face. Instead, she relaxed in his embrace.

"Thank you," she whispered and closed her eyes.

He closed his eyes as well and they both fell into sleep's deep chasm.

It was nine in the morning when Aphrodite walked into the kitchen. The warm aroma of freshly brewed coffee embraced her. She found Jane, sitting at the beige and brown speckled granite counter, eating a grapefruit.

"Would you like some breakfast?" she asked.

"I guess," Aphrodite replied.

"Let me get you some cereal," Jane offered, getting up from her seat. Jane walked over to the pantry and the door slid open. She pulled out a clear, empty container. “Oh. I forgot I ran out.”

“Don’t worry about it. I really wasn’t that hungry anyway,” Aphrodite lied. Her stomach growled in protest and she hoped Jane didn’t hear it.

“It’s no problem. It only takes a few seconds.” Jane took the lid off the container, walked over to the wall where there was a large, square-shaped hole. Jane placed the container in the hole and pressed a few buttons on the holographic key pad next to the opening. There was a soft hum in the room as Jane opened one of the cherry wood cabinets and took out a white ceramic bowl.

Aphrodite’s eyes widened with amazement as she watched her favorite cereal inexplicably appear in what was once an empty container. Jane removed the box and handed it to Aphrodite who was still stunned.

“Oh my God. How did you do that?” she asked as she inspected the container filled with Fruit Loops.

“Transporter. It’s fairly new technology so it’s not perfect. Sometimes the food tastes funny,” Jane explained.

Aphrodite picked up an orange loop from the container, sniffed it to make sure it had the proper fruity smell and then placed it in her mouth. Satisfied with its taste, she began to chew and smiled.

“Have they ever used it on people?” Aphrodite asked curiously, pouring herself a bowl of cereal.

“Yeah, but it’s not available to the public yet.”

They were interrupted by the patter of bare feet and Heath walked into the kitchen, yawning.

"Good morning," Jane said to him happily.

"Would you like some magic cereal?" Aphrodite offered him impishly.

"Is that like special brownies?" Heath asked.

"Better," Aphrodite replied.

"Cool. Hook me up," he said. Aphrodite poured Heath a bowl of cereal with milk. As he ate his cereal, his old injury decided to pay him a visit as his right arm surged with pain. Jane and Aphrodite could see the agony on his face.

"What's wrong?" Jane asked with concern.

"My arm's a little sore from helping Aphrodite the other day."

Aphrodite felt responsible as she remembered how Heath had pulled her out of the bin right before she would have been turned into nothing. Heath flinched when she put her hands on his shoulder and started to rub it.

"What are you doing?" he asked, his voice edgy.

"I'm massaging your arm," she said, bothered for having to state the obvious.

Jane stared at the unhappy couple, disturbed by their hostile behavior.

"It's so weird seeing you two like this. My mom and dad were never like this. They were happy together and couldn't keep their hands off each other."

Heath dropped his spoon in his bowl and said, "Thanks for the visual Jane. Now I can't eat."

Aphrodite removed her hands from his shoulder and flipping her middle finger at him said, "Eat this, Heath."

Heath looked at her, amused, while Jane could only shake her head.

"God," she said under her breath.

Feeling the early pangs of hunger, Aphrodite ambled into the kitchen hoping to find something sweet but instead she found Heath sitting at the counter eating a hotdog. She could tell by the look of pure contentment on his face, that hotdogs were just as delicious in the future as they were in their present.

"You know, those things can give you cancer," she warned playfully.

Heath grinned and replied, "I know. That's why I eat it with ketchup which has antioxidants. I figured I'd let them battle it out. I'm rooting for the ketchup."

"Go ketchup," Aphrodite said with a giggle. She was impressed that he knew and had correctly used the word antioxidant.

For a moment, Heath admired her smile which she rarely used in public or ever for that matter, as if she was rationing them. He remembered when she had worn braces for three years which they had given her hell for of course and when they finally came off, he thought she was just a geek with really straight teeth and continued to tease her. But in the few times he has seen her use it since their arrival in the future, he had come to realize she had a beautiful smile which seemed to transform her face.

She's kind of pretty, he admitted to himself.

Jane walked into the kitchen at that moment and said in a serious tone, "We should talk."

Jane felt odd sitting at the head of her walnut dining room table while Heath and Aphrodite sat across from each other. This was not the customary seating arrangement her family had established over the years. But then again, the circumstances were different. Her brother and sister were not present (Jane felt it was best), her parents were teenagers from the past, and the world was going to end for some unknown reason. Straying from tradition was the least of their problems.

"Do you guys have any more theories?" she asked them, as they brainstormed ideas.

"Zombie apocalypse," said Heath.

"Don't be stupid. Zombies don't exist," chided Aphrodite but then quickly looked to Jane for confirmation.

"They don't exist," Jane said with an amused shake of her head.

"How about a giant asteroid," Aphrodite suggested.

"Been there, done that. It was pretty exciting too," Jane said, remembering the thrilling broadcast from five years ago. The family had huddled together in front of the D.A.T.A. as they watched the holographic image of the asteroid hurtling slowly towards Earth. The asteroid, named Apophis, had come very close to hitting the Earth when she was about Heath and Aphrodite's age. Scientists had devised an explosive that caused the giant space rock to deviate from its direct path, safely avoiding their planet by several miles.

"Really?" Heath asked, intrigued.

"Yeah. We can't wait for the next one but they say it's not for another thirty-one years. If we ever get there." Jane added.

"A biological attack," Aphrodite said.

"We haven't had to worry about that either but if it were to happen, we're more than ready." A friend of hers who had connections had assured her that all the materials had been destroyed but the research remained.

"Terrorism," Heath said. It seemed reasonable that it would still be an issue in the future.

"That used to be a problem but it hasn't been for a while. Not that they've stopped trying." Jane said.

Heath's and Aphrodite's faces seemed to keep faltering with disappointment as Jane parried each verbal thrust.

"How's that?" Aphrodite asked, looking for details.

"Spheroid technology," Jane said proudly. "It's been the equivalent of fire or the wheel being invented today." Heath and Aphrodite looked at her blankly, unable to follow her explanation. Realizing this, Jane said, "Everyone carries one with them. Let me show you." Jane waved her hand over the D.A.T.A. "Spheroid's first test," Jane said to the silver wafer. The D.A.T.A. blinked to life as the holo-screen lit up like a Cyclops awakened by an intruder, its glow filling the room. As the D.A.T.A. prepped the requested video, Jane explained, "We used to have a big problem with terrorism, especially suicide bombers. At first they created technology that detected the explosives but they had no way to stop or contain them until recently. This is one of the first tests caught on video."

Heath and Aphrodite watched as the video showed what seemed to be several people in line at a bank waiting anxiously to be called by an available teller. Suddenly, a customer who had just come into view of the security camera, opened his coat revealing various explosives, wires and blinking lights wrapped around his torso. A woman, who was standing not too far from him in the queue, calmly removed a small object out of her pocket and rolled it toward the threatening man. The moment the small object made contact with his foot, he was instantly enveloped in a clear sphere. He blew up into thousands of fleshy pieces when the bombs detonated. But the now crimson stained sphere contained the explosion as well as the messy remains.

"Oh my God," Heath said, as his lunch crept up his throat.

"I think I'm going to be sick," agreed Aphrodite who was experiencing similar effects.

"Sorry. That's why they started to tint the spheres," Jane told them regretfully. But her parents continued to look ill. Jane remembered the first time she had seen the video but didn't have the same reaction because there had been previous footage that had shown far worse carnage involving innocent citizens. It was why Jane didn't flinch when the bad guy got what he deserved. Her parents used to not flinch either. "Maybe we should try again later," Jane said, looking at her nauseous parents.

Heath's queasiness passed and said, "But something's going to happen and if we don't figure this out soon, we won't be able to save you. I mean the future."

Jane took her father's hand in hers and said, "We can do this, Dad. And if we don't, you can keep coming back until you do. Right?" Heath looked at her as confidently as possible but he couldn't bring himself to lie to her and Jane knew it. She let go of his hand and said, "I might know someone who could help us."

"Can we trust them?" Heath asked apprehensively.

"As much as you can trust an ex."

"You have an ex-husband" Aphrodite asked, surprised.

"Ex-boyfriend," Jane corrected. "But I still consider him a good friend."

"What makes him so special?" Heath asked. Jane almost giggled. He sounded like a typical protective father.

"He's a scientist and he's done some work for the military. Maybe he knows something we don't."

Aphrodite hadn't met the man and yet she was already suspicious of him.

"What's if it's some secret project? What makes you think he would know something? Or would be able to tell you about it if he did?" She asked, challenging Jane.

"Because there aren't any secrets anymore. It's part of the agreement," Jane said matter of fact.

"What agreement?"

Jane exhaled slowly. Explaining the future to them was becoming tedious. They had more important things to do.

"Well, to put an end to the wars and the threat of a nuclear holocaust, most of the countries agreed to place all their cards on the table. Even the ones up their sleeves," Jane explained.

"I still don't get it," Aphrodite said, shaking her head.

"No one can do anything without everyone else

knowing. Every country has someone on the inside. It was the only way to build trust."

"You mean spies," Heath said simply.

"There is no need for spies. Not with the Global Alliance Supporting Peace."

Aphrodite looked befuddled and said, "G.A.S.P."

"Yeah, we were pretty shocked too when they came up with this agreement," Jane said. It was an accord most of the public still had doubts about but it seemed to be working for the moment.

"No, I mean the acronym spells G.A.S.P."

Jane laughed and said, "Well they had to change it when they realized the original agreement was C.R.A.P.P."

"Was it really that bad?" Heath inquired.

"It used to be Cooperative Regulatory Alliance Promoting Peace," Jane said, amused.

"That is C.R.A.P.P.," Heath agreed. "So what happens if a country gets caught cheating at poker?"

"They're put on the global naughty list where they'll be sanctioned up the wazoo. They're financially cut off immediately, their exports can't be sold and no one will do business with them. And, courtesy of the transport system, any leader who deviates from the agreement might find something annoyingly fatal where they least expect it."

Aphrodite couldn't decide if the world leaders had finally found a peace system that worked or new and improved ways to destroy one another. Either way, she was nervous.

"So you think he…" she began to tell Jane.

"David," Jane filled in the blank.

"David will help us?"

"I think so," she said, trying to sound as confident as possible.

"Are you going to tell him who we are?" Heath asked, uneasily.

"No. As much as I trust him, I don't know what he would do with that information," Jane assured them both. "Come on. He's not too far from here," said Jane, walking towards the front door.

11
Time flies

Walking the city sidewalks with Jane, the metropolis looked less intimidating to Heath and Aphrodite. They were actually able to appreciate the future architecture, seeing how the designers seemed to make sure there wasn't a mishmash of concrete structures invading one another.

Jane had just gotten off the comm with David, making sure he was okay with them stopping by. She smiled to herself as she observed her parents pointing to different buildings they still recognized and others that took their breath away. She enjoyed watching them as they took turns tapping each other's arm to get their attention, and pointing out the new points of interest.

They were nearing the Museum of Discovery and Science, which hadn't changed much, to their delight. Aphrodite was listening to the echoes of the balls clanking on the metal tracks of The Gravity Clock, which stood in the open-air atrium, and pictured the colorful balls winding through the colossal clock's rails as if being digested, when she suddenly became alarmed. Jane was approaching a copper plate, similar to the one Aphrodite had stepped on when she first arrived in the future and was nearly killed.

"Jane! Look out!" she shouted to her.

It had been years since Jane had last heard her

mother sound so distressed. She turned to look at her but by then her right foot was already stepping on the round metal plate. Aphrodite stared at her, bewildered, waiting for Jane to be kidnapped by a spheroid menace.

"What's wrong?" Jane asked her. Aphrodite's eyes were still wide with panic.

"You're stepping on that… I don't know what to call it but it makes a bubble that floats away and takes you to a garbage dump that fries you," Aphrodite spouted frantically, pointing at the plate accusingly. Jane put her hands on her mother's shoulders and could feel her trembling.

"Oh my God. Did that happen to you? Are you okay?"

"I'm fine," Aphrodite replied, feeling foolish. "Heath helped me," she added, smiling sheepishly at him. Jane smiled at her father, her grin inflated with pride.

Jane looked back to her mother and explained, "You're not chipped."

"Yeah, I pretty much walked away without a scratch," Aphrodite said, inspecting her arms. Jane laughed. Her parent's ignorance of the future was somewhat amusing.

"No, you don't have a chip. We all get one at birth. That's why nothing happened to me. It could see me. You two are like ghosts here. You don't give off any readings."

"Is that a bad thing?" Heath asked, his face heavy with concern.

"So far, yes. Hopefully that's as bad as it gets. Come on. We're almost there."

Jane led them into a massive quadrangle skyscraper that seemed to be made up of nothing but occluded windows. The shape reminded Aphrodite of a monochromatic Rubik's cube whose puzzle would never be solved.

They took one of the lobby elevators to the fourteenth floor, completing their trip in seconds. Heath had never experienced such momentum in an elevator and half-expected that they would continue to ascend, break through the ceiling and be told by Jane that they had just inherited a chocolate factory. The elevator doors opened before them unveiling a wide hallway crowded with people too occupied in their routine to notice them. They followed Jane to a door at the end of the hallway, watched it slide open and stepped through. The trio were greeted by a thin, scruffy looking man in his late twenties, who had been engrossed in a clear, plastic tablet, flipping through what appeared to be sheets of LED paper that would disappear as soon as he changed pages.

Aphrodite scrutinized Jane's ex-boyfriend. He wasn't much taller than Jane, his brown hair was unkempt and his looks were average at best, yet Jane looked at him adoringly. Her daughter could have done better and Aphrodite admired her for seeing past appearances.

David quickly put down the papers and said, "Jane. What a nice surprise. I'm so glad you came by." He walked over to her and embraced her warmly, hoping she wouldn't pull away from him after two seconds. He was relieved when she didn't.

"I know it's been a while and a bit last minute but I really wanted you to meet...uh...Elizabeth and Fitzwilliam," she said, gesturing to them. Afraid of revealing who they really were, Jane gave him the names of two characters from one of her favorite novels.

"Nice to meet you Elizabeth," David said as he shook her hand effusively. He released his grip and grabbed Heath's outstretched hand. "Nice to meet you, uh, Fitzwilliam." Heath could hear the disapproval in his voice and wanted to laugh.

"Yeah," he said, feigning humility. "My parents didn't love me so they saddled me with a strange name," he added with a wink to Aphrodite. She rolled her eyes with a heavy sigh and looked away.

"So, you said you need my help," he said, returning his attention to Jane.

Jane fluttered her eyes, gave him her sweetest smile and said, "I kind of dragged them down here by telling them that your job is really cool and you could help them with their science project." David was thrilled to have an opportunity to help and hopefully impress Jane. More than anything, he wished to restore their broken relationship.

"Sure. Do they know what their project is about?" he asked enthusiastically.

"The future of science. You know, major discoveries, possible experiments. That sort of thing."

As Jane and David conversed, Aphrodite strayed away from them to explore the lab. Heath followed her with his eyes as she strolled around the room, studying the large stainless steel tables at the center of lab, which held several Bunsen burners heating various bubbling beakers, percolating unknown substances. She was clearly impressed with the menagerie of equipment scattered throughout the area. A glass door to an adjoining room grabbed her attention and she began to amble in that direction but her brief expedition was interrupted by one of David's young lab techs, who stepped in her path. The young man was only slightly taller than Aphrodite. His white lab coat made his olive skin appear darker than it really was. He smiled pleasantly at her and began a conversation Heath couldn't overhear what they were saying. Instead, he tuned in and out of David's yammering as he observed Aphrodite interact with her new friend.

"They're doing something vital with nano technology…developing viruses that kill other viruses but are harmless to humans…a new energy source…a few steps away from controlling the weather…"

Heath watched with interest as Aphrodite took a few strands of her hair, and twirled them with her fingers, laughing as she exchanged words with the stranger.

Oh my God. She's flirting, he realized.

But even more surprising to him was that the stranger was responding to her amateurish signals. Heath saw the young man step closer to Aphrodite, clearly enchanted by her. Aphrodite appeared to be telling him a story, which Heath was curious to hear as well because she was waving her hands wildly. In all her excitement, she knocked something off the counter, shattering it into pieces that probably rendered it useless. Heath saw Aphrodite turn red and desperately mouth several apologies to the now angry man who dismissed her with a livid stare. Still flushed, Aphrodite moped back to Jane's side where Heath snorted, stifling a laugh. Seeing his smirk, Aphrodite glowered at him.

She and Heath both caught the tail end of David's rambling and Jane's wide smile when he said, "Oh, and we think we've found a permanent fix for cellulite."

Jane, Heath, and Aphrodite slowly made their way back home. The quiet trio, were each lost in contemplation, reflecting on their day. Miserable with being alone with her thoughts, Aphrodite was the first to break the silence.

"David seemed nice. Do you think he'll figure out who we really are?" Jane knew that it had been a risk taking them to meet him but, like so often in life, they were without a choice.

"He's pretty absent-minded so I don't think so. Oh, look out for the shoplifter."

Heath and Aphrodite looked in both directions of the sidewalk but neither of them saw the runaway offender Jane had warned them about. Jane pointed up at the sky and when they looked up, they saw a flying contraption hovering over one of the sections in a long line of storefronts. A clothing store called *Wear in the World*, began to lift from its base and rise in the air like a magician's assistant. The shop continued to rise, leaving the surrounding buildings untouched as if it had simply been a card pulled from the middle of a deck.

"Why is it stealing a store?" Heath asked.

"It's not stealing it. It's relocating it. The rent was probably too high in this area."

"Isn't it easier to just move everything into a new store?" Aphrodite asked, as if stating the obvious.

"How is that easier? Depending on the distance of the new location, that store can be reopened in as little as fifteen minutes and have a new store in its old spot before the day is over," Jane explained.

Heath and Aphrodite stared at her dumbfounded, trying to process a future where garbage floats, stores fly and yet they were walking.

They stopped at the curb and waited for an opportunity to cross the intersection. Jane stepped off first even though there was an incoming car traveling at a relatively fast pace. Aphrodite crossed after her, keeping a nervous eye on the speeding car.

Heath, who had been craning his neck as he watched the floating shop transform into a tiny blip in the sky, crossed last. But since most of his attention had been diverted by the flying object, he was not aware of the car. Aphrodite, halfway across, turned to see that Heath had not noticed the vehicle and it seemed the driver was oblivious to Heath as well because the car had not slowed down. It was going to hit him. Aphrodite ran to Heath, tackling him out of the car's deadly path, nearly causing him to hit his head on the curb. They both felt pins and needles from shock, as they fell to the floor, their noses bombarded by the smell of asphalt. The automobile sped right by them, not even a disgruntled honk from the driver.

When Heath realized what had almost happened he yelled, "What the hell? Why didn't that jerk slow down?"

Jane, who looked as if someone had opened a faucet and drained out her blood said repentantly, "I'm so sorry. That was my fault. I forgot you're not chipped."

"So? It doesn't mean that guy should drive like

an idiot."

Jane shook her head, more frustrated with the future than her parents.

"Most of the cars run on an autopilot program. They know to avoid other cars and people, but since you don't have a chip..."

"He's the invisible man," Aphrodite finished for her.

"Good thing Mom is quick," Jane said, smiling proudly at her mother.

"Thanks," Heath said to Aphrodite.

"No problem," she replied.

Heath lay in bed, his eyes watching the ceiling as stars seemed to wink back at him from above. Aphrodite lay next to him, ignoring Heath and the starry ceiling as she tried to fall asleep. It had taken them a few days, when they first arrived in the future, to realize that the reason why they didn't see a television in their room was because it hung over their heads. A few days after that, they learned the bare wall across from them served the same purpose.

On sleepless nights, they would try to watch T.V. shows or the news if they wanted to fall asleep faster. But most of the time, they didn't care for the programing. It seemed there wasn't anything to the watch in the future either. Instead, they would watch what were called *Dream Savers,* which were images that were usually dull enough to cure most cases of insomnia. One of Heath's favorites involved sheep jumping over a broken, wooden fence. His interest for it didn't stem from his need to count the sheep as they leaped effortlessly over the rotted railing. He would watch hoping one of them would eventually trip over the barrier. But tonight he wanted to sleep so he chose the twinkling stars as he tried to forget his close call with the car earlier that day. But he was struggling as it reminded him so much of his motorcycle accident and as the night wore on, he realized he didn't want to fall asleep. Although his nightmares had been few and far between recently, he was worried they would try to make up for lost time.

Determined to not fall asleep with his accident being the last thing on his mind, he tried to focus his thoughts on anything else. His brain agreed to change the subject but what it chose next, surprised him.

Before he could stop himself, he asked aloud, "I wonder how we fall in love?"

He was startled when Aphrodite answered, "By some miracle." He thought she had fallen asleep.

"Well you, I get. I'm popular, good-looking and sometimes even charming," he said with an impish smile.

"Wow," she scoffed, as she rolled over to scowl at him. "And yet I continue to resist you. But that's not what I meant by a miracle."

"What did you mean?" he laughed, unfazed by being rejected so openly by her.

Aphrodite let out a sigh as she tried to find the words and sat up in bed.

"I have a dead heart," she declared as if announcing a medical diagnosis.

"A what?", he scoffed as he sat up in bed.

"I don't think I'm capable of love. I mean I love my parents unconditionally even though I hate them but when it came to my boyfriends…" she shrugged her shoulders, "I don't think I ever loved any of them."

"Never?"

"I was attracted to them and enjoyed spending time with them but that's about it."

"And they never noticed or called you out on it?"

"Well, there was one," she stated softly. "He never said anything directly to me but I think he broke up with me to see how I'd react." Her voice was quiet when she added, "I think I disappointed him."

Heath stared at Aphrodite, dumbfounded. He was having a hard time wrapping his head around the idea that any guy would be heartbroken from losing Aphrodite. But it wasn't just that. He thought about his parents who had been married for more than twenty years and how the quality of their relationship had not diminished over time. He thought about his own heartbreak from a few years ago when his ex-girlfriend, Denise, moved to Jacksonville with her family. They had tried to stay together but they quickly discovered that what had been said about long-distance relationships was true and they mutually agreed to move on without the other. But it still took his broken heart almost as long as his injured arm to heal.

"Maybe you have a possum heart," he suggested.

"Excuse me?"

"You know, possums play dead when they're afraid or don't feel safe. Maybe your heart is just playing dead."

"I think your brain is playing dead," she said as she lay back down in a huff, pulling the thick covers over herself and turned away from Heath. For the next hour, she mulled over his words and wondered what could Heath possibly do that would make her feel safe long enough for her to develop feelings for him.

12
Turn Back Time

Aphrodite sat at the D.A.T.A., engrossed in a home movie she was watching. Days were slipping past them like a stealthy thief in the night. Their efforts seemed fruitless. To take her mind off the growing pressure, she made her searches more personal. She was unaware of Heath's presence until he pulled up one of the dining room chairs next to her and sat down. Her face reddened when Heath looked up at the screen. He was the last person she wanted to share front row seats with.

"I was looking through family photos when I found this," she explained, her voice barely audible. Heath's eyes were transfixed on the moving images of their wedding video. It was odd watching himself, in a black tux no less, slipping a ring onto Aphrodite's finger, her face a cascade of tears. His doppelganger wouldn't stop smiling.

"At first I thought I was crying because I was marrying you or pregnant or both but now I think I'm crying tears of joy," she explained as her face slowly returned to its natural color. "I've never had those before," Aphrodite added, unable to look at Heath.

He smiled at her, unsure if she could see him through her peripheral vision considering the thick curtain of hair covering her profile. He was tempted to brush it away but resisted. Instead, they sat in silence as the video cued from the beginning. Both of them jumped when Jane walked into the room.

Jane regarded the video for a moment and asked with a chuckle, “Are you watching that again? Isn’t that like, what, your sixth time today?”

This caused Aphrodite’s face to flush as if she had sat in the sun all day after basting in baby oil and then allowing a three-year-old to apply rouge to it. Heath had never seen such a shade of red before and was amused. He thought it was endearing.

Aphrodite left her seat to stand by her daughter.

“You had a beautiful wedding,” Jane said dreamily.

“It looks expensive. Where do you think we got the money because I know it’s not from my parents,” Aphrodite wondered.

“Don’t you know?” Jane asked, as if Aphrodite should have known the answer to her own question.

Heath fidgeted in his seat and changed the subject by asking, “You wouldn’t happen to have any videos of me playing football, would you?”

“I wish. You used to talk about it all the time,” Jane said wistfully.

“God I miss playing. We were awesome too.”

“Here we go,” Aphrodite said, rolling her eyes.

“Did I ever tell you about Tyler Bale? He was one of the best receivers I ever played with.”

Jane could only smile. She hadn't seen her father this excited since arriving in the future and didn't want to tell him that she had been hearing about Tyler since she was five years old. Instead she shook her head, inviting him to repeat the story she already knew by memory. But Aphrodite had no interest in humoring Heath.

"Could you please stop talking about football?" she demanded. Heath looked at her indignantly. He opened his mouth to protest but Aphrodite continued, "Tyler Bale couldn't catch a bus, a cold or a cold on a bus. And don't get me started on your offensive line. They couldn't block a view." Heath was too stunned to argue but Jane smiled broadly, having heard this before too. She began to think there was hope for them after all.

"You saw us play?" he asked Aphrodite.

"Oh yeah and I would have to say my favorite part always involved you at the bottom of a five man pile up," she said wistfully.

"I thought I saw you at some of the games," he recalled. But instead of confirming what was obviously true, Aphrodite seemed to backtrack.

"Well, I only went to a few games. Two or three of them really."

"You like football," he accused playfully.

"No. I just have a deep appreciation for strategy, teamwork and athleticism," she countered. Heath and Jane stared at her, her words meaningless to them. "Fine.

I like to watch men bash into each other violently and make grunting noises," she finally conceded. Heath couldn't believe he and Aphrodite actually had something in common.

"Then you must like hockey too," he assumed.

Aphrodite looked rather abashed and said, "No." After a few seconds she added, "The uniforms aren't tight enough."

Jane laughed and, remembering she had an appointment soon, looked at her watch.

"Oh crap!" Jane exclaimed and quickly covered her mouth, realizing she had just cursed in front of her parents. "Sorry. I have a doctor's appointment in two minutes," she explained to them.

"Why don't you just cancel it? You might as well reschedule if you're not going to make it on time," suggested Aphrodite.

"I'm not late. There's still so much I have to show you. I should be done in half an hour. See you later," she said as she walked to her room.

Aphrodite sat back down next to Heath where they stared in awkward silence at the blue glow of the holo-screen.

"What's your favorite team?" Heath asked finally.

"The Baltimore Ravens," Aphrodite answered, not having to think about it.

"Really?"

"I read a lot of Edgar Allen Poe. How about you?"

"I always wanted to play for the Colts," he replied, thinking about the jersey he had bought at a sporting goods store two years ago. It was the closest he would ever come to representing his favorite team.

Aphrodite blindsided him when she said, "Cool. They used to be a Baltimore team too."

Heath smiled, impressed with her knowledge and said, "That's right." He looked hesitantly at her, wavering on a question he wasn't sure he wanted her opinion on or not. He couldn't understand why it would even matter to him but decided to ask anyway.

"What did you think of me as a quarterback?"

Aphrodite puckered her lips in thought and said, "You didn't suck." Her real opinion was that he had been an exceptional player and, had it not been for his injury, would have eventually gone pro in a big way. But, much like a chubby child, his ego did not need any extra feedings.

"I didn't suck?" he repeated.

"There are three categories of quarterbacks. Sucks, doesn't suck and Dan Marino," she said, counting off on her fingers.

"Marino?"

Aphrodite's eyes narrowed.

"Don't tell me you're one of those people who think you need a ring to be the best. His record speaks for itself," she told him huffily.

"Well a ring doesn't hurt and most of his records have been broken," he countered.

"Because he had a knife in a gunfight and still set those records."

Heath chuckled, truly enjoying the discussion. It was probably the first time he didn't mind being alone with her.

"Your boyfriends must have loved talking to you," he commented. Her facial expression hinted at the opposite.

"Not really. Guys that are into football aren't into me and guys that are into me aren't into football."

"Oh," he said to himself, as if it should have been obvious.

They shared an awkward silence that seemed to last longer than their conversation. Ever since he had found the pen, Heath's mind seemed to be jumbled with conflicting thoughts and the person he had detested for so long was the only one who could help him sort them.

"After we fix things here, I've been thinking about using the pen to go back and prevent the motorcycle accident and I wanted to know…"

Knowing where the conversation was going, Aphrodite interrupted him and said, "It's a terrible idea, Heath. If you stop that accident, who knows what else you might change."

"But it's just one thing," he pleaded.

"I know it's not exactly assassinating Hitler or saving the Titanic but one thing in the past could change five or even five-billion things in our present. Maybe the changes are harmless, but I don't think you should risk it."

"I was just wondering," he said, his voice fraught with disappointment. Heath stared sulkily at the D.A.T.A.'s blank holo-screen.

"What if you were supposed to be in that accident? Maybe it had to happen so that you would find the pen," she said, trying to convince him it was the right thing to do, yet she felt guilty. There had been hope in his eyes when he talked about changing his past and she of all people was an expert on losing hope. She considered that they were about to attempt the improbable in changing the future. If they succeeded, maybe they should take it as a sign and attempt the impossible. "Maybe if I went with you, I could help you not make a mess of things," she told him.

Heath looked at her. Hope had returned to his eyes along with shock.

"You'd do that?"

"You had...real potential until your accident. I didn't care at the time because I really hated you and thought you deserved it," she confessed, "but I see how much it means to you and why should we both be miserable."

"Maybe when we go back, I can tell myself to be

nicer to you."

She considered it for a moment. If it were even possible, and he did manage to alter his past behavior thereby even changing the way his friends treated her, it might help her avoid years of verbal and emotional torment. She might even end up a happy, well-adjusted person. *Nah.*

"That would be nice but, I really think we should change as few things as possible," she declined. An uncomfortable hush fell upon them until Aphrodite asked, "Since we seem to be playing twenty questions, can I ask you something?"

"Go for it," he said, assuming he was more curious about her question than she was about his answer.

"What's up with you and Amber?"

"Why do you ask?" he said with surprise.

"Well, you spend a lot of time together but you're not dating which is kind of weird."

"Why is it weird?"

"She's beautiful and I guess you're pretty too so, it would make sense. But sometimes, when we're in the cafeteria and you guys aren't looking, I sit there and imagine an out-of-control school bus crashing through the wall and plowing down your table and I've noticed you ignoring her while she stares at you like a piece of key lime pie."

"Key lime pie?" he laughed as he detected a hint

of nervousness in her statement.

"Key lime rocks."

"She is pretty," he agreed. "And I was into her when we first met, but she's high maintenance. And kind of annoying. What is it about pretty girls being so annoying? I mean, you're not."

"But I'm not pretty," she reminded him.

"You're not ugly," he mumbled grudgingly. Aside from her hair and acne, there seemed to be some other changes about Aphrodite, Heath couldn't put his finger on. She seemed to be getting prettier with each passing day and he couldn't understand how. It reminded him of a story his English teacher discussed in class last year, about a man who remained youthful while his portrait grew more gruesome. He began to wonder if Aphrodite had a hideous picture, hidden away in the attic of the Bailey house.

"I'm not ugly," she repeated as if tasting the words in her mouth. "You know what? It's the nicest thing anyone has said about me so, I'll take it. Thank you." Again, silence seemed to be intruding their conversation until Aphrodite asked, "Is there anyone else?"

Heath considered telling her about the red-head from the antique store but realized he couldn't remember where he had placed her number and had no intention of looking for it.

"No," he answered. "Besides, I've been too

depressed lately to be any fun," he added truthfully. There had been countless girls he could have easily pursued but he couldn't stop feeling sorry for himself long enough to establish a relationship and would slowly drift away after a few dates.

"Ah, depression. My old friend," Aphrodite stated. "Glad to see we share a mutual acquaintance."

Heath watched as Aphrodite turned back to the holo-screen, her fingers dancing over the holographic keyboard as she typed in a few words and began a fresh search that would hopefully be useful to them.

"So…who's your second favorite quarterback?" he asked. Aphrodite grinned.

Jane watched her parents from the darkened hallway, observing their interaction. She had used the ruse of a doctor's appointment to leave them alone and hid in the shadows. Their conversation wasn't as audible as she had hoped, but when she managed to overhear enough words to realize they were still discussing sports, her high spirits tumbled to the ground.

How are these two ever going to fall in love? she wondered. They were finally less hostile towards each other but there was something still missing. One of the biggest red flags was the fact that not once had she heard Heath utter the nickname he had given her mother. She couldn't remember when he had started to use it but she knew that it was Heath who nicknamed her mother *Love*, inspired by the goddess she was named for. She worried if their coming to the future would change that forever. She decided she would have to settle for the fact that at least he was no longer muttering the word witch, whenever Aphrodite left the room. After a few minutes, Jane sighed quietly and went to her bedroom.

Aphrodite sat at the edge of the disheveled bed, an avalanche of tears rolled down her face as she sobbed quietly. Unable to suppress her anxiety and feeling ashamed, she had been hiding there for the last half hour. She and Heath had been in the future for weeks now, they were no closer to finding the truth, and she was panicked. She heard the hiss of the bedroom door as it slid open and Heath walked in.

The door closed after Heath stepped through the threshold. He stood still, startled to find her crying. In all the years he had known her, he had never seen her shed a single tear not even when they ridiculed her. The bed dipped as he sat down next to her and put his arm around her back, stroking it gently. She leaned into him and rested her head on his chest. Heath did his best to ignore the sweet smell of Jasmine that drifted off her skin.

"What happened?" he asked with alarm, feeling the tremors of her sobs. Part of him didn't want to know the answer. She was the strongest person he knew yet something had her rattled. That wasn't good.

"We haven't found a damn thing and we have

less than a week to figure this out. And I'm frustrated because I can't slam that stupid door," she yelled, gesturing to the bedroom door.

"We can do this," he said, trying to sound convincing.

"But what if we can't? I really like Jane. Even if she wasn't my daughter I want to protect her from whatever is about to happen. Where is she anyway?" she asked through stuttered sniffles.

"She went to run some errands."

"Oh. That's good. I don't want her to see me like this," she said, sounding more composed. Suddenly aware of Heath's proximity and her more than likely unflattering appearance, she sat up and began to clear away the salty streaks from her face.

Seeing that she had missed a few tears, Heath placed his hands on her face and used his thumbs like wipers to clear away the remnants of her misery. Aphrodite watched Heath's face wordlessly as he did this, too disoriented to move. His thumbs finally became still and she assumed he would release her and leave. But instead, he leaned forward and kissed her forehead. His lips continued to follow an erratic path, leaving soft kisses in its wake along her face and jaw line. Aphrodite's heart raced each time his lips came close to hers, teasing them with the promise of something more.

"What are you doing?" she whispered.

"Comforting you," he answered without

stopping.

"I… may need a lot of comforting," she replied faintly.

Heath finally stopped and looked at her intently.

"I can do that," he said huskily.

She welcomed his lips on hers as she wrapped her arms around him. They kissed fervently, the gravity of their embrace pulling her closer to him. Heath stopped suddenly and they both stared at each other, as if communicating an unspoken question between the two of them-*Do we really want to do this?* Spellbound by his eyes, which were like forests of green skies, Aphrodite forgot the question while Heath answered it when he tenderly placed his lips back on hers. Void of the previous urgency, the moment had taken a gentle turn.

Kissing Aphrodite had never exactly been on Heath's bucket list, but six days ago, when they had been sitting together at lunch, she had tossed her head back when she laughed at one of Jane's childhood stories. It was in that moment when he became possessed with the need to touch and kiss her. The feeling kept building up inside him with each moment he spent with her causing him to become tongue-tied at times which was a new experience for him. The few opportunities he wanted to fulfill his longing, he was sure she would rebuff him. But today was different. He didn't care if she rejected him. His desire to try outweighed his fear of failure.

Aphrodite's head swam with questions. As much

as she was enjoying the experience, she wondered why Heath had initiated it in the first place. Was it a mercy kiss or was he just desperate? Maybe it was an end of the world snog or he was fantasizing about Amber. Lost in their intimacy, Aphrodite helped Heath remove his shirt. Despite his arm injury, it was obvious he had continued to maintain his athletic physique which Aphrodite felt when her hands slowly explored the length of his muscular arms, starting at his wrists and then resting them on his defined chest. He was a god but she was a goddess in name only. Even when she had despised him, she had always been aware that, by society's standards, Heath was a desirable man, just never to her… until now. Recently, she would find herself mentally tracing his chiseled jaw line, stopping at his dimpled chin only to start all over again. She would also think about his full lips, which seemed inviting, causing her to lose all focus though thankfully he had never noticed.

Even sleep didn't always release her from this rest-depriving curse. At night, she would lie awake, overly aware of his nearness.

All of her insecurities that she had thought were dead and buried were rising from their graves, wanting to eat away at what little self-esteem she had left. Her arms couldn't decide whether to push him away or pull him closer. She finally shoved doubt out of the driver's seat and succumbed to desire.

They were both startled when they heard Jane's

voice calling out to them.

"Mom! Dad! I'm back with dinner."

They both started, looking panicked.

"Crap," Heath panted.

"Quick. Put this on," she said to him, tossing him his shirt. They both stood away from the bed and Heath was dressed by the time Jane opened the bedroom door. Jane noticed that her parent's faces were flushed and both seemed to be slightly winded.

"What's going on?" she asked suspiciously. Based on their appearance, she already knew the answer but she hoped they would confirm what she suspected.

"Nothing. We were just… jogging," Aphrodite told her.

"Yeah, we were jogging around the room," Heath agreed and quickly ran in place as a demonstration.

"I could come back later if you need more time to jog," Jane said mischievously.

"No. I'm good," Aphrodite answered mortified and left the room. Heath looked hurt and confused as he watched her leave.

Jane noticed that he was wearing his shirt backwards and inside out.

"You may want to fix your shirt," she said, tugging at the tag playfully. He looked down and saw the tag that had betrayed him. He turned his back to her and removed his shirt. As he was flipping it outside in, Jane touched the left side of his back lightly.

"Where's your scar?" she asked, sounding stunned.

Putting his shirt back on quickly he replied, "What scar? I've never had a scar back there."

"You had this huge scar on your back. It looked like numbers or something but you didn't like to talk about it. Weird." Seeing that this version of her father didn't want to talk about it either, she left the room.

"Weird," he repeated to himself.

Heath and Aphrodite lay uneasily in bed, their backs to each other. Aphrodite's hand nestled underneath her pillow as she struggled with her muddled emotions. The uncomfortable silence reminded Aphrodite of when she had accidentally walked in on her parents fooling around and neither one of them could look or talk to her the next day which had been just fine with her. But the ghost of their kiss haunted her and she needed answers to exorcise it.

"Why did you kiss me?" she blurted.

"I don't know. Why did you kiss me back?"

"I don't know," she said, echoing his answer. "Do you think it was because of the stories Jane's been telling us and the wedding video?" she queried.

Heath knew what had triggered his affections earlier and it went beyond stories and old home movies. When he wasn't thinking about their dilemma, he found himself thinking about her, which was more often than not. In the few weeks they had spent together, he discovered he could easily read her yet he felt there was more to discover and hoped he would. But he wasn't ready to tell her that.

"Maybe," was all he could say.

She chewed on her bottom lip as she tried to decipher his one word answer.

"I was thinking. Maybe our future turned out the way it did because you asked me to come with you. Maybe if you had asked Amber instead, she would be Jane's mother," she told him. The thought of anyone else being Jane's mother, unsettled her and she clutched the pillow tighter to her head. She felt the mattress shift as he rolled over to look at her.

"You don't believe in fate?" he asked.

Aphrodite couldn't tell if he sounded surprised or hurt. Maybe it was both.

"It doesn't matter. I'm letting you off the hook. When we get back...if we get back, I don't want you to think you're obligated to be with me."

"Could you please turn around and look at me," he pleaded. Aphrodite was tempted to give in to his request.

"I'm afraid that if I do, looking won't be enough." She also didn't want him to see the traces of fresh tears.

"I know what you mean," he agreed.

"And we really can't afford any distractions. Not

with an apocalypse looming around the corner."

"Do you want me to sleep on the sofa?" he offered.

"No. This isn't that distracting."

"Maybe for you," he chuckled darkly. Aphrodite smiled as her tears continued to temporarily pool on the pillow which were subsequently swallowed by it.

13
Out of Time

Aphrodite and Jane sat at the D.A.T.A., scanning various news articles on the holo-screen. Jane's hands moved as if she was conducting a symphony, cycling through various images with the flick of her hands. Nothing they saw seemed threatening or end of the worldish, which would seem like great news to anyone but them. They were almost out of time.

"Do you think we'll figure this out by tomorrow?" Jane asked apprehensively.

"I hope so or we're all out of tomorrows," Aphrodite answered, unable to meet her daughter's eyes.

"You can always go back and try again," Jane suggested encouragingly.

Aphrodite winced, still averting her eyes. With so little time left, she didn't want to spend it giving bad news to Jane but there didn't seem a way to avoid it.

"I don't think so. Not anymore. By coming back, we might run into ourselves, creating a paradox. We have to get it right this one time."

Jane's eyes narrowed.

"But Dad said…" she started, but Aphrodite quickly cut her off.

"He doesn't know. I haven't had the heart to tell him." Aphrodite finally looked at Jane. She had never been prone to discussing her feelings but again, time was short. “Jane. I want you to know, just in case...”

“Please don’t do this, Mom,” Jane interrupted, her voice cracking, but Aphrodite was determined.

“Let me finish. I want you to know how proud I am that you’re my daughter.” It was the first time Jane had heard her mother acknowledge their relationship aloud and it touched her.

“I’m proud to be your daughter, too,” Jane smiled.

Aphrodite looked at Jane admiringly, and said, “You’re so beautiful. You get your looks from your father.” It always astounded her how Jane’s eyes were nearly the same shade of olive green as Heath’s.

“Really? Last night he told me I got them from you.” Aphrodite placed her hand on Jane’s shoulder.

“Oh, Jane. Your father is weird that way.”

“He looks at you differently,” Jane stated.

“What? Like I have three heads instead of five?” Aphrodite teased.

“Like you’re the only person in the room.”

Apocalypse or not, Aphrodite didn’t want to have this conversation and squirmed in her seat.

“He’s just a little confused because I can quote football stats. Besides, am I supposed to be impressed that he’s willing to look at me now that I’m not hideous anymore?” she said, sounding offended.

Jane looked and sounded ashamed when she said, “I cheated.”

"Huh?"

"Well, when I first met you and saw how much you guys disliked each other, I kind of sped things up," Jane said guiltily.

"What are you talking about?" Aphrodite asked, confused.

"Dad married you the way you were not the way you are. But when I saw how bad things were between the two of you and I knew you were going to make the changes anyway..." Aphrodite's inner turmoil surfaced. Her estimation of Heath, which she had built over the years, had slowly deteriorated in less than a month.

"Do you love him?" Jane asked.

"I don't hate him anymore," she answered vaguely.

"That's not exactly heartening," Jane said, sounding irritated.

"It's complicated."

"Well uncomplicate it because even if you do save the future, I won't have one if you two don't get together," Jane said angrily.

Aphrodite hated herself for causing her daughter pain, but she didn't want to lie to her.

"I wish I could promise you that. Heath and I have become closer. Closer than I never imagined," she said, her face slightly blushing as she recalled the heated kiss they shared the other night. "But this is the Twilight Zone and I don't know how either one of us will feel when we get back to our time," she said frankly.

Jane opened her mouth to say something else on the subject but Heath walked into the room, causing them both to drop the topic.

Aphrodite's heart skipped a beat when she saw him and wondered if it might be a delayed side effect from the time travel. She would have to ask him later if the same thing was happening to him.

"Anything yet?" he asked, oblivious to the tension that had not quite dissipated from the room.

"Not really. The things we've found have already happened or they're scheduled after our D.O.D.," Jane answered.

"D.O.D.?" Heath repeated.

"Date of doom," Jane clarified.

"Nice. Any other ideas?" The room filled with the sound of a phone ringing, causing Heath's question to be left unanswered. Heath and Aphrodite had been in the future long enough to know that Jane was getting a call. Jane touched a button on the D.A.T.A and was surprised when she saw David's smiling face appear on the holo-screen.

"Hey. I hope I didn't catch you at a bad time. I wanted to see how the science project was coming along and if my help was still needed," he said.

"Not so good. We haven't figured it out yet," Jane told him.

David seemed pleased and said, "Good, cause I

think I have something for you guys that will knock your socks off and get you an A."

"I'm not sure we have the time," Jane said frowning. But David was determined.

"Sure you do but you have to come now or it'll be too late." Jane looked to her parents for their approval, which they gave with an uncertain nod of their heads.

"We'll see you soon," Jane told David and ended the call.

14
Time bomb

David greeted his guests heartily as they walked into the lab. He was sincerely happy to see Jane again, as well as Heath and Aphrodite. His excitement was evident to the three of them as soon as they saw him. But his eagerness stemmed from more than just seeing his ex. He had something to show them and the anticipation was surging through him like a livewire. He was positively giddy.

"I'm so glad you made it. You're going to love this," David told them.

"What is it?" Aphrodite asked, curious to know what could cause a man to act like someone who had found the true whereabouts of the Holy Grail. He had a secret and he was dying to share it.

"The ultimate discovery and you're going to be witnesses to it."

"Is it something you invented?" Heath asked, getting swept up in David's zeal as well.

"I wish," David answered wistfully.

Jane scanned the lab looking for David's surprise but she didn't see anything she hadn't already seen before.

"Where is it?" she asked him.

"We're going to have to go on a little field trip for that," he said with a smirk. He gestured for them to follow and led them into his office. It was a small room that contained a mahogany desk with an inactivate D.A.T.A. wafer lying upon it, and a few leather chairs. David led them past his desk, to the rear wall and stood in front of a long clear tube, which ran from the floor to the ceiling.

"I don't understand," said Heath.

"It's a transport. Like Star Trek," Jane explained.

Aphrodite noticed the opening in the tube. An opening that was large enough for a person to step through.

"You mean… and we…and then…no. I am not getting in that thing. I don't want to taste funny," Aphrodite babbled.

"What?" David chortled.

"They're nervous because they've never used a transport before," Jane told him.

"Of course they haven't. Only the lucky few have, but I promise that it's perfectly safe," he said, sounding certain.

"Is this the only way to get to where you want to take us?" Heath asked, looking just as frightened as Aphrodite.

"Yes. So let's stop wasting seconds before even the transport won't get us there in time," David advised, his enthusiasm slightly evaporating.

Heath and Aphrodite looked to Jane for assurance. She smiled at them but her eyes didn't seem to be in agreement with her mouth. She was scared too. They would just have to chance it and hope David's invite led to the answers they had been searching for.

David expected for them to be eager at getting the opportunity to use the transport when only a select few had been given the privilege, but he would have to settle for resigned.

"Great. You won't regret this. I already programmed it so all we have to do is step into it one at a time. Ladies first," David said as he grabbed Jane's hand and helped her step into the transport. Heath and Aphrodite looked on nervously, not knowing what would happen next.

"I'll be fine," Jane promised them, fidgeting in the narrow tube.

"Try not to move. It helps prevent, uh, accidents," David warned, not wanting to alarm them further.

A calming female voice filled the room and announced, "Passenger detected. Prepare for journey. Five, four, three, two, one." Jane's body seemed to dissolve before their eyes, as if being removed like a human stain. David smiled at Aphrodite, pleased with the awe plastered on her face.

"Next."

Heath felt his whole body tingle as it reintegrated within a transport capsule that was not in David's office.

He was somewhere new and Jane and Aphrodite where there waiting for him, smiling as if they had just survived bungee jumping off the Grand Canyon, both high from the experience.

Heath stepped out of the transport and looked around the room. He saw several translucent capsules similar to the one he was just in. He guessed he was in a transport room. Just outside the room and down the hallway, he saw what looked like a huge screen with an image of the earth and walked over to it.

Placing his hand on the screen, he asked, "Cool. Does this get E.S.P.N.?"

David must have just arrived because he answered the question.

"That's a window."

Heath's mouth fell slightly agape.

Pointing at the window, Heath said, "If that's a window, and that's the earth, then what's this?"

"Lunar Base Titus."

"Lunar? As in moon?" Aphrodite asked, her voice heavy with awe.

David nodded his head vigorously, delighted with their reactions.

"Welcome to Project Zwicky," David announced theatrically, his arms spread out like a ringmaster announcing the start of the circus. "Follow me," he said to his three guests and led them to a large expansive room filled with dozens of people in white lab coats milling around holo-screens and other busy machinery. Several yards away, stood a largish metal box whose blinking lights reminded Heath of the winter carnival. A few scientists stood around the humming machine, for some last minute computations.

Aphrodite thought they had stepped into a television show. It even had a live studio audience when she noted the stadium style seats which lined the walls, filled with fellow scientists and politicians from around the world, eager to see whatever they were all there for.

What are they here for? she wondered.

The star of the show was Dr. Spinnaker, a tall, gangly, white-haired man who was barking orders to the people around him. But what also made him stand out from the others was that he appeared to be a luddite. Unlike his tech crazy colleagues, he wore a monocle and a pocket watch as if anything else would be too advanced for him. The odd man smiled when he saw David and welcomed him and his three companions.

"David. Glad you made it. You brought guests?" he asked, eyeballing Jane, Heath, and Aphrodite.

"Yes, let me introduce you. Dr. Spinnaker, this is Jane, my um… an old friend of mine, and this is Fitzwilliam and Elizabeth. They're working on a science project and I thought they might find this useful."

"Useful? This will be man's greatest gift" Spinnaker scoffed. The odd scientist excused himself and joined a small group of associates who were discussing last minute preparations.

"What's going on?" Aphrodite asked David.

"It's the event of a lifetime," he replied animatedly.

"What is it?"

"Well, if everything goes well, they will be tapping into the perfect energy source that is clean and limitless," David explained, but his tiny tour group looked unimpressed.

"How?" Jane asked.

"Dark matter," he simply stated. The three of them understood the words dark and matter but when put together, they held no meaning for them and stared at David blankly.

"What's dark matter?"

"Something that is everywhere yet can't be seen," David responded.

"How do you turn something you can't see into energy?" Jane asked.

"They're using satellites and the earth's magnetic poles as a source for a field to spin atomic particles," David answered, hoping his explanation was simple enough for them to understand.

Heath and Aphrodite looked at each other briefly, as the same thought popped into their heads.

"Okay. Now, in English, could you tell us if this experiment could be dangerous?" Heath inquired.

David's lips seem to shrug when he said,

"Anything can be dangerous but I really don't think there is any threat here. These people are the best of the best and they've taken every precaution imaginable."

"Why wasn't this made public knowledge?" Jane asked suspiciously.

"Because several attempts have been made in the past and they failed each time. It's no longer newsworthy to the media but I have a feeling today will be different."

Heath wondered how David could guarantee that but before he could ask, Dr. Spinnaker interrupted by saying, "We're about to begin. Why don't you guys stand over there. You'll have the best view," he said motioning to a small area just outside the center of activity. The room was warm with nerves and anticipation. All eyes were on Dr. Spinnaker, rapt with attention.

Jane snuck a glance at David and snickered silently. He looked like a teenager about to see his first R-rated movie.

Dr. Spinnaker turned to his assistants and asked, "Are we ready?" When they all gave their consent he commanded, "Turn on the Zwicky."

His co-workers began to press holographic buttons and the equipment began to hum a soothing, tuneless song. A large holographic screen displayed a gauge that showed the amount of dark energy that had been collected in the few minutes the Zwicky had been active. The scientists seemed quite content with the quantity of matter they had amassed in a short amount of time.

A klaxon suddenly drowned out the humming from the Zwicky, which troubled the scientists.

Jane, Heath and Aphrodite looked at each other anxiously. The only thing they could comprehend about the situation was that something not good was happening. Heath and Aphrodite wondered if this was what they had traveled to the future for.

"We've got a black hole," one of Spinnaker's assistants announced, sounding more disappointed than distressed.

"How bad is it?" Spinnaker asked calmly.

A holographic image of the black hole appeared before them. The dark object was encircled by three large satellites, that seemed to shrink with each passing second.

"Small enough for us not to feel anything yet. But at its rate of growth, no one will be feeling anything anymore in three minutes and fifteen seconds."

Spinnaker sighed deeply, displeased with their defeat yet again.

He hung his head and ordered, "Shut it down."

"What is it? What's going on?" Aphrodite asked David.

"It's a black hole. It's the one side effect of tapping into dark matter they were hoping to avoid," he said flatly. "Looks like another failure," he sighed.

"Can they stop it?" Jane asked panic stricken.

"It should disappear once they shut down the program," he explained, his voice as even as a tranquil lake.

They took their cue from David and relaxed a bit until they overheard one of the scientists exclaim, "It's not working!"

Spinnaker grabbed the man's lab coat and demanded, "What do you mean it's not working? It should have decayed by now!" Realizing that he would need the help of every viable mind in the lab to prevent the eviction of the entire human race from the universe, he released the man whose name he never learned and doubled his determination to stop the greedy monster that was growing out in space.

"We need to do something!" Aphrodite shouted at Heath.

"Fine. You distract them and I'll unplug it," Heath replied sharply.

"I can't believe it. We finally know what it is and we can't stop it," her voice cracked with emotion. Jane's eyes welled up with tears, realizing how hopeless the situation was. Even with a time traveling pen, they couldn't use it now to escape.

"You can't go back, can you?" she asked her parents. Heath shook his head somberly. Teary eyed, Jane reached out to her parents and pulled them to her in a hug. She could accept her fate but it wasn't for them to share.

"I'm so sorry," she cried. Heath and Aphrodite held their daughter to them and waited for the yawning maw to swallow them whole.

"Blow the satellites!" Spinnaker yelled over the din of the klaxon.

"But that will set us back ten years," a female colleague, Dr. Williams, protested.

"We won't have ten years if you don't blow those damn satellites!" Spinnaker roared, his face red with rage.

Dr. Williams turned away obediently, and began the process for terminating the satellites.

The anxious audience watched the holographic image of the black hole that appeared to be growing in the room with them, with breathless anticipation. The three satellites that surrounded the expanding void, exploded one at a time as they received the command to self- destruct. There was a collective sigh of relief when the massive monster disappeared, finally slain. The klaxon immediately ceased its clamor as if it had been shamelessly crying wolf the whole time. The dejected audience, who had been watching the experiment, began to vacate their seats and make their way to the transport room.

The siren suddenly started screeching a new warning. The scientists looked at the readings, thinking another black hole had formed but what they saw was worse than that. The spectators who had been trickling slowly towards the transport room began to push and stumble over one another as their need to leave the moon became imperative. Jane, Heath and Aphrodite ran up to Dr. Spinnaker to investigate the latest catastrophe.

"What now?" Jane demanded.

"The D.M.E. is about to blow. The event overloaded it. The container was supposed to purge itself once we aborted the experiment. If the Dark Matter Extrapolator explodes, it's taking the whole base with it," the scientist explained gravely. He looked just as frightened as they did.

"What about the transports?" Heath asked.

"Not enough time or capsules to evacuate everyone," Dr. Williams interjected.

"You guys have got to be the stupidest geniuses I've ever met!" Jane accused them angrily.

Aphrodite, annoyed that their lives had been endangered twice in five minutes and fearing the second time's the charm, was determined to save their lives.

We can't use the transports and we can't use the pen, she eliminated from her head. *What do we have?* she asked herself, looking around the room. Her eyes settled on Jane as she remembered the video involving the spheroid. "Jane. Do you have one of those bubble things with you?"

Jane's forehead creased.

"Yeah, sure," she said, taking one out of her

pocket.

"How big can it get?" Aphrodite asked

Understanding her mother's plan, Jane smiled and said, "Big enough," and placed the small sphere in her mother's right hand.

"Which one's the D.M.E.?" she asked Spinnaker. He pointed to the large piece of machinery in the distance, whose blinking lights and whining had become more pronounced. Judging the distance, Aphrodite knew there was no way she would make it.

She turned to Heath, offered him the sphere and humbly said, "I throw like a girl. You're going to have to do the honors."

Heath was taken aback by her gesture. He wasn't sure whether he should be flattered or annoyed that she had passed on the responsibility of saving everyone on the lunar base.

"My arm…" he said uneasily as she carefully placed the sphere in his hand. She felt guilty for burdening Heath with their fate but he was the only person she trusted enough to succeed.

"You can do it. Just pretend its Travis Bale which shouldn't be too hard because that thing can't catch either," she said, a smile playing on her lips.

"You only have to hit it. It does the rest on its own," Jane assured him.

The D.M.E.'s whining, grew louder as it warned them they were running out of time. It was now or never.

Heath quickly estimated the distance, cocked back his arm and sent the small ball flying through the air.

The sphere thudded when it hit its target and enveloped the D.M.E. The machine's complaints were muffled for a few seconds before it finally exploded in the confines of the inflated sphere. The muted blast caused the base to shudder slightly and a few people to lose their balance and fall to the ground but there was no damage to the building. Those who had been unable to escape the base erupted into applause and tears of relief.

Several scientists patted Heath on the back and congratulated him, reminding him of what it felt like to throw the winning touchdown. But he was glowing from a new feeling that easily eclipsed the one in his memory. He embraced the two women he had come to love, grateful something had finally gone right.

Waiting for David, Jane and Aphrodite stood with Heath in the transport room. They were all eager to finally leave the place that had almost become their tomb. Heath noted that mother and daughter seemed to be sharing the same morose frown.

"What's wrong with you guys? They stopped the black hole and we saved everyone on the base."

"That's the problem. Without us, they still would have stopped the black hole but the base would have exploded. It would have killed everyone on the moon but we don't think it would have affected the earth," Jane explained glumly.

“So this wasn’t it?” Heath asked exasperated, his head on the verge of imploding. They had risked their lives only to discover they were still at risk.

“No, this wasn’t it,” Aphrodite confirmed.

15
Time Bandits

"We've run out time," Aphrodite announced grimly when they had all transported safely back to David's office.

A perplexed David, who was still oblivious to the world's lack of future asked, "What are you talking about? We have plenty of time."

"Our science project. Looks like we're getting a failing grade," Aphrodite appended. David contemplated her words for a moment.

"Well, if your teacher lets you turn it in late, I might have something for you myself," he offered eagerly.

"That's wonderful David. What is it?" Jane said half-heartedly. She felt culpable that he would never live to see his endeavor. None of them would.

"I don't want to jinx it," he told her nervously.

"Oh. Well then I guess you'll tell me how it goes," she said, aware that call would never come.

"Of course I will," he said keenly, looking forward to the day he could show her. It had been years since he had been directly involved in something he felt was worthy of being called momentous. His continuous failures and determination to overcome them had caused him to drift away from Jane, but if all went well his name would forever go down in history and hopefully, in

Jane's heart as well. David's D.A.T.A. signaled an incoming call.

"I got to get that. Do you guys mind?" David told them, gesturing towards the doorway. Jane smiled at him and David left them alone in his lab.

Aphrodite strolled through the lab aimlessly as they waited for David to finish his call. Her nerves were in shambles and Heath could see it on her face as he watched her. Aphrodite's hands glided across the silver counter tops as she walked past them, careful not to break anything this time. She had orbited the room a few times and grew tired of its familiarity, thinking that this must be what it feels like to be a goldfish. She remembered the small room she never got the chance to explore and hoped it would have something that would help get her mind off the hopeless situation.

At first glance, she thought it might be a storage room. Though its door was open, she peered through the room's window to get a better look and saw a few innocuous items, a white mouse in a cage and something that made her breath catch in her throat.

Not wanting to look away, she kept her face pressed against the window and asked, "Heath. Do you still have the pen?"

"Of course I do," he said reaching into his back pocket and produced it. He walked over to Aphrodite holding out the evidence but she never acknowledged it.

Jane, who knew her mother very well, could tell

she was distressed.

"What's wrong?" she asked approaching Aphrodite.

"Look over by the mouse cage. What do you see?" she urged, her words creating a small formless fog on the window.

Heath and Jane both mimicked Aphrodite's prying posture and saw a white mouse running on its wheel. When their eyes moved to the right of the cage, they saw what had troubled her. In a small, clear storage case was a red herringbone fountain pen.

Heath gasped.

"Oh my God. Do you think…" Instead of finishing his thought, Heath went into the room and removed the twin pen from its case.

"What are you doing?" David asked suddenly. The three of them jumped at his voice, unaware that he had walked in.

"Where did you get this?" Jane demanded angrily.

"That? It's just a pen. Could I have it back please?" David said firmly.

"Where did you get this, David?" Jane repeated.

"Give me back my pen!" he bellowed, holding out his hand. His face was reddened with ire, his temples threatened to burst due to the veins that now pulsated.

"We can't do that," Heath said defensively. David scoffed.

"What do you mean you can't do that? You're going to give that back to me now!" David's open hand was now a fist as he looked to each of their faces. His eyes which had been narrow with rage, suddenly widened with realization. "You know what it does."

"More than you know," Heath replied, confirming the scientist's suspicion.

David smiled cynically and said, "Then you can imagine my surprise when one morning, I made a belated journal entry and as soon as I wrote the previous day's date, I suddenly spotted another me in my office."

"What kind of man keeps a journal?" Heath snickered.

"It's a research journal," David corrected. He began to pace the room. The woman he loved and a couple of kids were going to ruin his greatest achievement. Like so many times before in his life, science came first. He shoved aside all his emotional attachments to them and explained, "At first I thought it was a clone and it was part of some huge conspiracy so I left before he...I...saw me. But when I began to look for any clues about what was happening, I realized I was reliving the day before. After that, I was able to piece together the puzzle of the pen."

"How did you get it?" Aphrodite asked coldly.

"I found it in a box when I moved out of Jane's place."

Aphrodite's jaw dropped.

"What do you mean you found it in a box when you moved out of Jane's place?" She looked crossly at Jane. "You lived with your boyfriend? We are so talking about this later."

"But Mom," Jane protested, "I'm twenty four-years-old."

"I don't care!" Aphrodite turned her attention to Heath and punched his arm. "You hid it in a box? Are you kidding me?"

"It wasn't me. Not yet," Heath said, rubbing his arm. Aphrodite may claim to throw like a girl but she definitely didn't punch like one.

"What's it to you anyway?" asked David, tired of the interrogation.

"It doesn't matter," Heath told him.

David stared down Jane and the two teens who she seemed to share several facial characteristics, though they claimed to be distant relatives. David's knees nearly gave out on him when he realized who Jane kept bringing to his lab.

"Oh my God. How could I be so stupid? How many times did I see your faces at the condo?" he said, remembering the pictures of their older versions on Jane's dresser.

Jane went up to David and put her hand on his shoulder.

"You have to understand why we lied to you," she said to him.

"And why we can't give the pen back," Heath added.

"I can't let you do that," David refused.

"Why?"

"Because I plan on impressing some very important people."

"With how you can travel through time?"

"Why would I want to travel through time when I could control it?" David scoffed.

"What are you talking about?" Jane asked, her voice quivering. Her insides felt as if they had been transported out of her and had been replaced with dread.

"I'm talking about freezing time. Isolating it in specific areas..." he replied self-importantly. "...and the mouse is going to be the first test subject."

Jane, Heath and Aphrodite sensed movement at the lab's entrance. They looked over and saw five uniformed security guards with their guns drawn.

"You triggered security when you removed the pen," David informed them.

Heath grabbed Jane and Aphrodite and pulled them behind him in a vain attempt to shield them.

Approaching the frightened family, one of the security guards said, "We'll take it from here."

"Wait," said David, holding up his hand. The five men stopped and watched David walk up to the detainees. Because he had his back to them, the sentries didn't see that David had removed two pens from

Heath's hands instead of just one. David turned away and signaled the guards to remove the three trespassers.

"You can't do this David! You're going to end the world! Whatever you're planning, you're going to end the world!" Jane screamed as they were removed roughly from the room. David stood speechless, her words of warning stuck in a loop inside his head.

Feeling defeated, Jane, Heath and Aphrodite sat on the floor of the makeshift cell they had been placed in. It was a bare office that had never been used; its four unblemished walls still pure white. Jane sat in a corner, her head resting against the wall, wondering when David had become evil. Her parents sat close together, feeling bleak.

"I can't believe this is how it ends. And we're stuck inside this stupid room," Jane yelled, slamming the wall with her fist, leaving a small bruise on her knuckles.

Heath was aware that they had finally stumbled across the reason the future would end tomorrow, but he couldn't comprehend why.

"I still don't understand what's going to happen," he confessed.

"David is going to use the pen to freeze time. And I don't think he's tested his little theory yet, but when he does, it's going to work, but it's going to affect everyone," Jane explained.

"You mean no more time?"

"No more time, no more future," Aphrodite answered miserably.

What the room lacked in décor, they made up with silence.

"I forgive you," Aphrodite said calmly to Heath.

"For what?" he asked her, wondering how he had wronged her this time.

"Everything. Everything you ever said to me and whatever you would have said to me if things had continued." If they were going to die, she wanted Heath to know she no longer loathed him. In fact, her feelings about him had changed quite a bit, but end of the world or not, she couldn't bring herself to say the words aloud.

Since she seemed to be saying good-bye, Heath thought this would be a good moment, probably the only moment, to speak his mind. He wanted her to know how he had stopped dreaming about his motorcycle accident since the first night they shared a bed as if her presence kept the nightmare at bay. He also wanted her to know that his biggest regret was not being able to live out the events he had seen through the videos and pictures. His list went longer than that but with time running out, he wasn't sure where to begin.

"Aphrodite, I…," he began to say but was interrupted when the door slid open and David, an African-American woman in a military uniform and two armed guards walked in. Jane, Heath and Aphrodite rose to their feet. Judging by her demeanor and the amount of medals that decorated her blue coat, the woman appeared to be in charge. Her skirt was surprisingly short for a woman of her stature. Even her tall black heels seemed out of place. But there was not denying that the men in the room were intimidated by her.

General Denise Carter was a four star general who had no patience for anyone who might threaten Project Cryos. As it was, the project's secrecy had been breached and a universal agreement meant nothing to her considering the magnitude of their newest discovery. David had told her who the trespassers were but she had to know how these three people had managed to discover what they had hidden from every country in the world.

"It has come to my attention that we had a few special guests and I wanted to meet you personally. Why are you here?" she said, her voice feigning civility.

"Why should we tell you?" Heath answered, his voice poisonous with hostility. General Carter's red painted lips hardened.

"Because if you don't, this room will become crowded when we bring in the rest of your family." She focused her glare on Jane and said, "Mary and Apollo, correct? Now answer my question."

Jane's face blanched. The trio felt betrayed that David had revealed enough about them to put the rest of their family at risk. They were going to have to cooperate if they wanted to protect the absent siblings but their reply became unnecessary because David intervened on their behalf.

"They had a pen of their own and wanted to see the future but they lost their pen in the process. That's why they came here. They found out about ours and wanted to steal it to go back to their time," he informed the general.

Jane didn't know what to make of David's lie. It appeared no one in the room could trust him.

"Amazing. Two time-traveling pens," she said in awe. "I wonder if there are any more out there. It's a shame they lost theirs. We'd have twice the power," the general marveled, her dark face glistening like a fresh pot of coffee, under the harsh fluorescent lighting. She turned her attention back to Heath and Aphrodite and asked, "So, what do you think of the future so far?"

"I think it sucks almost as much as you do," Heath spat out.

The general smiled scornfully and said, "You must be the clever one."

"Why are you doing this?" Aphrodite implored. The general thought about how much of the question she was willing to answer. She was certain that escaping the room would be impossible for them and telling the truth might be fun for a change.

"Because we can. We finally have something the other countries don't have," she gloated.

"What about the peace agreement?"

The general laughed. She thought the peace

agreement was the greatest illusion ever conjured up that would disappear at any moment. The United States must be prepared for such a scenario.

"Everyone knows its crap," the general stated harshly.

"I thought it was G.A.S.P.," Heath corrected but the general ignored him.

"How do we know other countries aren't secretly trying to dominate the rest? It's like every country has been handcuffed but everyone has a key. If we've managed to hide this experiment, imagine what they've hidden from us. But don't worry. We'll let the world know as soon as we're successful."

Jane gaped at David.

"I can't believe you're a part of this. This is not like you," she said to him.

"With this discovery we'll be able to invade a rogue country without spilling blood," he rationalized. He couldn't understand why Jane, of all people, didn't see him as a hero.

"But we're the rogue country," she argued.

The general intruded on their exchange by asking, "Do you really believe that another country in our position would show more consideration in regards to this new found technology?" When no one responded to her not so rhetorical question, she smiled with satisfaction and added, "I didn't think so. If it makes you feel any better, we're not looking to start a war. Just increase our chances of winning one."

"Wow. That's world class stupid," Jane remarked without a hint of sarcasm.

Aphrodite had grown tired of the general's lack of morality, intelligence and mute button. There was something they needed to discuss that was bigger than a hypothetical war.

"Listen, lady," she began to say but David cut her off.

"How dare you speak to General Carter that way!" he chastised.

But Aphrodite only rolled her eyes and said, "Whatever, General lady. You seem not to understand something. You..."

David slapped her face, cutting her off.

Heath lunged at David but his fist failed to make contact with the scientist's face when the armed guards cut off his assault. Heath stepped back angrily and rejoined his family. Jane was tending to Aphrodite, who was still rubbing the large red handprint stamped on her right cheek. Her streaming tears seemed to magnify the welt on her face. His fists clenched, Heath vowed to himself that as soon as the moment presented itself, David would know her pain.

Unmoved by the incident and eager to test the pen, the general felt it was time to leave.

"As much as I've enjoyed meeting you all, we must be going."

"I'll join you in a minute," David told her.

The general sighed with disappointment. She hated delays but they couldn't conduct the experiment without him. She would allow him a few more minutes with his "friends."

"Will you be all right?" she asked him, her eyes on an irate Heath.

David walked up to one of the guards and removed a Taser-like device from his belt. The short man parted with his weapon dutifully.

"I will be now," David said boldly.

General Carter approached the keypad by the door, pressed the code that unlocked it and left the room, taking the two guards with her.

As soon as the door closed, Aphrodite yelled, "Idiots!"

Ignoring her, David pocketed the Taser. He opened his mouth to speak but Heath slammed it shut when he punched him in the jaw.

Rubbing his aching chin, David muttered, "I'm sorry for slapping her but I couldn't let her tell the General what you're up to."

"Why?" Jane demanded.

"Because if they knew about your pen or thought you're a threat to the project, I wouldn't have a chance to do this," he said and removed their pen from his lab coat pocket and offered it to Heath who looked at him warily. "I didn't want them to know about it. Take it back and get out of here. I'll take care of Jane."

Heath reached out cautiously for the pen, and exhaled with relief when he had it back in his possession. But this small victory meant nothing compared to what they had ahead of them. "We can't leave yet," Heath told him.

"Why not?"

"Because even if we use the pen to get out of here, this building isn't in our past. And this isn't over."

"The end of the world?" David asked dubiously. He had been replaying Jane's words inside his head but he was struggling to believe them.

"Why do you think we came all this way for? Did you really believe your own lie?" Aphrodite questioned. If David believed them, then it would mean the end to his project and his chance at prominence within the science community.

"I would like to think you're mistaken," he admitted. Jane gently rested her hand on his bruised face.

"David, they came to save us. There will be no future if you go through with your experiment."

Perturbed, David stepped away from Jane and slapped his forehead several times with the palm of his right hand. After the third cranial thump, he lowered his hand and faced his indicters once more.

"Is that why I couldn't travel into the future?"

"We think you're going to succeed in stopping the flow of time but you won't be able to isolate it.

Frozen time will become a universal constant."

"And it will be frozen forever," Aphrodite warned him.

He finally absorbed the veracity of their words. His head swam at the thought that he would be responsible for single handedly assassinating mankind.

"Oh, my God! What have I done?"

"Nothing. Yet. Please help us," Jane begged, her voice warm with empathy.

"Of course but what can I do? Getting near the other pen will be next to impossible."

"Not for you," Jane pointed out.

"Even so, I can't just walk out with it. Especially now. They've moved up the test. It's in half an hour," he said, his voice heavy with despair. The small surge of hope they had felt earlier when they realized David was willing to help them, quickly died out. They only had thirty minutes to save the world and they didn't even have a plan.

"Okay, then we get out of here, go back to our time, destroy our pen and all this will be over. Right?" Heath proposed but David disagreed.

"I'm not sure it'll be that easy," David argued. "This pen has properties that we can't even begin to understand. There's no guarantee that it will cease to exist in the future when you return to your past. It might not even be the same pen. We can't take that risk." He considered telling them about the possibilities of a parallel universe but he decided the Wells family had dealt with enough crazy for one day. As it was, Heath was having a hard time wrapping his mind around the idea of a second time machine.

"Are you kidding me? What are the chances it's a different pen?" Heath asserted.

"If you go back and you're wrong…" David trailed off, giving himself goose bumps as if he could already feel the chill of eternal stagnation. Aphrodite examined the keypad, a scheme forming in her head.

"I have an idea but first I need the code to open this door," she told David.

"Three-two-five-one-one-three," he dictated.

"Three-two-five-one-one-three. Got it," she said, committing the code to memory.

"What's the plan?" Heath asked her.

"We can't escape this room because it's guarded...today."

Heath grinned in spite of himself. Something he had come to admire about Aphrodite was her tenacity and how her dark eyes blazed like burning onyx when she was inspired, like she was at this moment.

"Cool. What then?" he asked without reservation.

"We'll travel back one day, steal the other pen and then jump back one more day. We should then be able to just walk out of here."

David admired Aphrodite's coolness under

extreme circumstances. But her plan needed some tweaking.

"Make sure when you take the pen that you write fast or run faster. Security won't take long to catch up to you. Even if you two aren't chipped," he advised.

"Thank you," she said, grateful for his help and the fact that he truly loved Jane enough to risk everything. She had no doubt he would keep her daughter safe if they managed to escape.

"Just remember I helped you if you should meet me again," he joked.

Aphrodite turned to Jane, whose eyes were moist, not wanting to face the inevitable.

"We have to go now," she said, forcing her voice not to crack. She blinked her eyes, fighting the moisture that was trying to surface.

"I hate that I have to lose you again. But at least I get to say good-bye this time," Jane said, unashamed of her tears. Jane hugged her mother, not wanting to let go. Aphrodite was surprised by her emotional attachment to the woman she had known for barely a month. Now she couldn't imagine her life without her.

"Stay safe," Jane told her, ending the embrace with a kiss on her mother's cheek.

Jane hugged her father next, squeezing him with all her might. She had always adored her father, admiring his quiet strength and devotion to his family. He was her measuring stick when it came to men and she had yet to meet anyone who was his equivalent. David had been the closest and based on his actions today, he had closed the gap slightly.

Heath held his daughter, afraid to let go.

"We'll see you again. I promise," he told her, hoping it wasn't a lie.

"I can't wait," she sniffled. She kissed her father's face, and then stepped away from him. Their farewells complete, Heath handed Aphrodite the pen, which she gladly took from him.

"Let's do this," she said, removing the top off the pen and wrote yesterday date's on Heath's arm. They heard the scribbling sound, felt the pull of the past and disappeared. When they reappeared in the room, it was exactly the same except David and Jane were no longer there, as if they had never existed. And it was more painful than they had anticipated, not having Jane at their side. Aphrodite went up to the keypad and inputted the code to unlock the door. The door slid open and they walked out of the room. They found themselves in a busy hallway where there were no armed guards and no one looked at them like escaped criminals. They navigated the network of corridors and easily made it back to David's lab without incident. They went straight to the door that separated them from the pen but the door was locked, complicating things.

"What are you two doing?" they heard a familiar voice ask. They turned and saw David standing just outside the threshold of his office, looking stern.

"It's like déjà vu," Heath muttered to Aphrodite.

She chuckled nervously and said, "We saw your cute rat there and it looked lonely so I thought I might pet it."

"Lucy's a mouse who needs to be left alone. But I'll tell you what. In two days, when she's more famous than Mickey, I'll let you be the first to touch her," he said, taking a few steps towards them, obviously upset. He didn't want them anywhere near the pen and it was unnerving for them to see his ambitious nature again.

"Thanks." Aphrodite replied ironically.

"Is there anything else?" he asked, his tone hinting it was time for them to leave.

"Oh. Jane's downstairs with a gift for you," Heath blurted, hoping to buy more time.

"A gift?" David reiterated.

Picking up on Heath's cue, Aphrodite said, "Yes. A big one too and she needs help bringing it up."

"Why didn't you help her?" David addressed Heath.

"He's weak," Aphrodite said, elbowing Heath.

"Yes, I'm weak," Heath agreed mechanically.

"Well I'm really impressed that Jane is downstairs with a big gift for me considering I just got off a call with her. Now what's really going on?"

Heath and Aphrodite looked at David uneasily. What should they tell him?

"Well, you see…" began Aphrodite but David cut her off.

"I'm no longer interested. I'm calling security."

He started towards the wall near his office, where there was a switch that would summon security but he paused when Heath said, "Please don't! We can explain but you probably won't believe us." Preoccupied that Heath would try to attack him, David never saw Aphrodite sneak up behind him and smash a glass beaker on the back of his head, knocking him out cold.

"Did you really want to explain it to him again?" she asked.

"Not really," he replied appreciatively.

Aphrodite knelt down by David's unconscious body and said with some satisfaction, "That's what you get for almost ending the world." She stood up, preparing to walk away but then quickly returned her attention to the unmoving body and blurted, "And for living in sin with Jane."

Amused, Heath asked, "Feel better?"

"Getting there," she said, the experience cathartic for her. "What are we going to do about the door?" she asked him, remembering it was locked.

Heath examined the keypad and realized that it wasn't a keypad at all. He picked up David's limp body, dragged it to the sealed door, used his fingers like prongs to pry open David's eyes and waited patiently as the optical scan recognized the scientist's identity, opening the door to them.

Impressed, Aphrodite asked, "How did you know?"

He shrugged his shoulders and said with feigned modesty, "C'mon. Everyone knows about optical scans." They stepped into the insignificant room and located the pen, which was still poorly ensconced in the clear box. Heath placed his hand on the container's lid, ready to lift it.

"We need to be quick," Aphrodite reminded him.

"I know," he said and removed the pen from its plastic prison. They knew they had triggered the alarm the second they had opened the container but they weren't too concerned. The plan was to grab the pen, use it to travel back one more day and then walk out of the building, which wouldn't be on high alert at that time. Heath uncapped the pen, placed the nib on Aphrodite's arm and began to write yesterday's date. That's when they hit the snag.

"It's not working." Heath said, his calm demeanor fading fast.

"What do you mean it's not working?" she asked, staring at her blank arm which should have had a written date by now. Aphrodite snatched the pen from him and tried writing on his skin but it refused to release its ink. She unscrewed the pen from its center only to reveal an empty barrel. It had no ink sac.

They both heard commotion coming from David's office.

"Damn! They're using the transport! We need to get out of here now!" Aphrodite yelled urgently. She screwed the pen back together, handed it back to Heath and they both ran out of the lab. They headed for the elevators hoping the heavy traffic of people in the hallway would help slow down their pursuers. But when they heard a bell chime, signaling the doors were about to open on their floor when neither one of them had pressed the button, they chose to find another exit.

"The stairs!" Heath shouted, pointing at the stairwell. They ran down the stairs hoping neither one would trip or collapse from exhaustion. Heath had never been one for prayer but today he had a lot to say to God. Hopefully he didn't ignore lapsed altar boys. After what felt like hours of running, they reached the bottom floor and discovered that there were two doors, one of them leading directly outside. They pushed open the door marked with a small red sign, which read "Street access" and stepped into dying daylight. Aphrodite felt safe on the sidewalk, which was teeming with people who had come very close to becoming permanent fixtures where they ambled.

She grabbed Heath's arm and said, "I think we're okay out here," and slowed their run to a brisk walk.

The building they had fled suddenly dispensed

several armed soldiers into their vicinity. The two teens broke into a run but were afraid they would never be able to elude the guards. As they ran, Aphrodite remembered something about the area. She grabbed Heath's hand, desperately trying to ignore the warmth of his touch and the thrill it sent up her spine and led him towards the site, hoping her plan worked. She found her intended target and purposely stepped on the copper plate that had given her several bad dreams since their arrival in the future. A huge, clear sphere enveloped the couple and they slowly rose into the air.

"Take shallow breaths," she told a dazed Heath, as she struggled to take her own advice. It was a difficult task considering how much they had just ran. The sphere seemed even smaller to Aphrodite as she was sharing it with Heath this time. Even though he was kneeling, the sphere's low ceiling forced Heath to awkwardly bow his head.

Trying not to breathe heavily, Aphrodite pressed her face to the bottom of the sphere and squinted her eyes, hoping she would be able to spot something familiar. She studied the landscape as they passed over it. Aphrodite thought about her glasses again and this time she was glad she didn't have them on because she was self-conscious of her appearance whenever Heath was around. They drifted for several agonizing minutes before she spotted the object of their salvation. The sphere took them to the same dumpster she had fallen into when she had been kidnapped by the orb that had ambushed her. That meant they were at least half way closer to the house. If their luck continued to hold out, it would take the guards a while to find them, especially when they didn't have chips to track.

As soon as they reached the garbage bin, gravity took hold of them after the bubble let them go. They fell into the large bin, with only a sparse number of trash bags to cushion their fall, which weren't as soft as they would have liked. Remembering how everything had been incinerated the last time they had been there, Heath leapt up quickly, grabbed the rim and pulled himself up as Aphrodite helped by grabbing his legs and boosting them. He balanced his body precariously on the edge as he reached for Aphrodite and raised her to the lip, which she grabbed as soon as she was within reach. They toppled over, both landing on their hindquarters. They got to their feet and started to run away when a thought occurred to Heath.

"Wait a second," he said to Aphrodite. He removed one of the pens from his pocket and tossed it into the container behind them.

"One down," he announced, looking anxiously at Aphrodite.

They continued their escape through neighborhoods and back roads, unsure if they were still going in the right direction. They just wanted to elude their pursuers they could relocate the Bailey house.

Every once in a while, Heath would insist they find an obscured spot to rest. Although he was tired, it was Aphrodite he was worried about. She looked like she was about to fall over from fatigue and they had no way to rehydrate themselves. Their latest stop was a neighborhood where they ducked behind a large oak tree. Heath peeked around the wide trunk to make sure they still weren't being followed. He recognized the corner house with the garish flowerbed from when he went chasing after Aphrodite and realized that there were now even more flowers as if they were reproducing or preparing for an invasion. He estimated the Bailey house was less than a mile away from them.

"We're pretty close. You need to start writing," he told her. He removed the pen from his pocket and handed it to Aphrodite. She took it from him, removed the cap and touched the point to the skin of his arm. But when she tried to record their return date, the nib was dry.

"Damn it, Heath! You got rid of the wrong pen! This is the one without ink!"

"Damn it!" Heath shouted, wishing he had thrown himself into the bin instead of the pen. They didn't have time to go back to see if it hadn't been incinerated yet. They had come so close and he screwed it up, just like his football career. He looked at Aphrodite remorsefully. There weren't enough apologies in the world that could fix this.

Unless. "Write on me," he commanded.

"I just told you, we don't have any ink," she argued.

"Use the point to carve it in my skin and hope the magic's not in the ink."

She looked at him as if he had just told her to euthanize a puppy. A month ago, she would have willingly staked him in his non-existent heart with the pen. Now she couldn't bring herself to scratch him with it.

"I can't do that. I can't hurt you," she protested.

"You have to!" he commanded. She recoiled at his severe voice. He had never yelled at her before and Heath saw the hurt in her eyes right before she turned her gaze to the ground. He understood her refusal, considering the physical pain she would have to inflict.

Calmly he said, "You're not really hurting me if this saves us." Aphrodite refused to meet his eyes. He placed his hand under her chin, gently lifting her face. "I'd offer to switch places with you but we'll be stuck here for sure if I have to do it," he murmured. Aphrodite stared at him for a moment.

"Okay," she agreed, her voice barely audible.

He removed his shirt, tossed it into the shadow of the tree, and turned away from her. "It'll be easier on my back," he said, offering it to her. Heath braced himself for the impact but what briefly brushed up against his back were Aphrodite's lips. She then pushed the pen's nib into his skin, drawing blood. Heath shrieked in agony as Aphrodite carved the first number. She withdrew the writing tool, unable to continue. "Don't stop! You can apologize to me when we're back in twenty-fourteen!"

Aphrodite resumed the arduous task of engraving the date when something suddenly caught their eyes. A few of the garbage plates that lined the streets started to rise from the asphalt, revealing transport tubes beneath them. They heard the whirring sound of them being activated.

"They know where we are," she fretted.

"Run!" Heath yelled, grabbing her hand. They were able to put some distance between themselves and the law enforcers who were just regaining their corporeality.

They soon ran past the house that had been painted plaid when they had first arrived in the future. Heath tried not to stare at it because it now alternated between the images of grinning, dancing bananas wearing top hats and the words "Eat Me," written in large, block lettering, scrolling across the house like an LED display.

Heath and Aphrodite glimpsed the lush, green hedges that marked the entrance to the Bailey house property. They reached the mouth of the pathway, ran up to the front door, expecting it to swing open as if it had been waiting for them expectantly but when Aphrodite tried the handle, she discovered it was locked. They had forgotten that in the time they had been gone, the caretaker of the house would have discovered the door unlocked and rectified it. Aphrodite dragged Heath to the rear of the house, his back trickling with blood, and prayed her way of entry had remained undiscovered. She pressed her hands against the window pain and lifted it open. They both climbed inside and quickly shut it closed.

"You have to finish," he told her.

She wiped away the oozing blood, smearing it until it was a thin layer, so she could see what she had started, and continued to etch the date into his back. They both heard the commotion of approaching harried voices and heavy footsteps just outside, followed by the sound of wood splintering as the police attempted to smash through the front door.

Aphrodite completed branding Heath with the vital numbers but nothing happened.

"It didn't work," she whimpered. She had damaged him for nothing. Heath's face glazed over with dismay. They had lost. They were about to be arrested, General Carter would get the pen back and the future was back on the chopping block. He wasn't ready to lose. Not this time.

"The old date! Did you scratch out the old date?" he asked, remembering the rules for time travel. They looked at his arm, which still had the date Aphrodite wrote on him when they had escaped detention. They heard the sound of more splintering wood and trampling feet coming from the next room. He howled with pain when she used the pen to slash across the old date, leaving a crimson line of blood and mutilated skin. Several armed men barged into the kitchen as the sound of scribbling filled their ears. Heath and Aphrodite disappeared and when they rematerialized, they were alone in the kitchen once again. They both shuddered, overcome with relief. Heath went to the sink, turned on the cold water and alternated between splashing it on his face and drinking it from his cupped hands. Aphrodite gaped at his seeping wounds. Scarlet stripes dashed down his back, staining his pants.

"Let's get you home and clean you up," she told him coolly. Heath shut off the water, not bothering to dry his face.

They both made their way to the window, and snuck out like a couple of intruders breaking into the world.

16
Back in Time

Heath winced as Aphrodite dabbed a large cotton ball soaked in hydrogen peroxide on his wounds, which seemed to drown out the metallic scent of copper in the air. They were sitting on his bed where there was a growing pile of bloody cotton balls. Aphrodite had bandaged his arm and the pain was subsiding. Using first aid tape, she fastened a large sterile gauze pad over the gory inscription. When Heath realized she was done tending to his wounds, he slowly put on a dark, loose-fitting, long sleeve shirt to conceal it from his family.

When he was dressed, Aphrodite instructed, "Get the hammer."

Heath picked up the heavy instrument that he had procured from his father's steel gray toolbox, and the blood-smeared pen they had used to get home. He laid the pen on his desk, took a deep breath and proceeded to smash it into several pieces. It felt therapeutic to destroy the object that had brought him nothing but chaos since coming into his possession.

Satisfied, he looked to Aphrodite and asked uneasily, "What do we do now?"

Ever since they had arrived back to their time, Aphrodite had pondered the same question. And being back in their reality, there was only one answer.

"Well, it's like we never left. So maybe we

should just act like nothing happened."

"Is that what you want?" he asked, trying to meet her eyes, but Aphrodite's focus was on the debris scattered on the desk's surface. Absentmindedly, she used her right index finger to shift the broken pieces of the pen. She briefly wished it was still intact so she could disappear into any time that wasn't this one. She couldn't bear to look at him.

"I think it's what's for the best," she said, barely audible. "I'll see you around," she added quickly and bolted for the bedroom doorway, swallowing the words she really wanted to say.

It had been three days since they had returned to the year twenty-fourteen and just as Aphrodite suggested, they both acted as if nothing had happened. Heath spent the weekend with his friends, hoping that would help him decompress, but by Sunday night, his restlessness had become intolerable. He assumed it was because he was returning to the life he had wanted to flee. But deep down, he was really dreading his math class and for once, it wasn't because of the material.

Heath and Aphrodite sat at their assigned seats, squirming uncomfortably. Aphrodite had returned to blanketing herself in her over-sized uniform. To the unobservant eye, things appeared to be back to normal, with Heath and Aphrodite seemingly loathing each other. Even Aphrodite's hair and face had begun to revert to their former appearance, just less pronounced. It was as if Jane had cast a spell on her from the future and it was now broken. Unfortunately for her, the nanites had lost their signal when they traveled with her to the past, and no longer functioned.

There were a few times during class where Aphrodite had been tempted to talk to Heath, but didn't know what to say. She considered asking him for paper or a pen but the latter almost made her burst into hysterics. The torturous hour seemed to crawl slower than a snail with a limp. They both silently prayed for the bell.

At lunch, Heath sat at his usual table, surrounded by his ignorant friends. He would never be able to tell them what he had endured to save them all. He was almost jealous of their naiveté, considering the new batch of bad dreams that had been waking him up in the middle of the night.

Having scarfed down a slice of pizza, Mike kept tossing a hacky sack in the air to keep himself occupied. Aphrodite sat alone and their routine was complete. But there was one small change to her behavior. She kept stealing glances of Heath, which had not gone unnoticed by Amber. She began to pout when she caught Heath looking over at Aphrodite with a look Amber wasn't familiar with. Something wasn't right and she was determined to fix it.

"Oh my God, Heath," she said loud enough for her friends at the table to hear. "Aphrodite keeps looking at you. She finds a hairbrush and some Clearasil and thinks she can stare at you now."

"Now she's delusional too," said Omar Alvarez, one of Mike's friends whom Heath had come to recently dislike. It seemed to have become a recurring theme among Heath's circle of friends. Since his return from the future, he had come to realize he was surrounded by jerks.

Always willing to please Amber, Mike asked, "You know what I miss right now?" Everyone at the table looked at him expectantly, knowing something good was about to happen. "The carnival," he announced, answering his own question. Positive there were no faculty members present, Mike stood up, beamed the footbag at Aphrodite's cold drink, causing it to pour all over her. Aphrodite sprang up from the icy shock, dripping with humiliation.

Heath struggled with his desire to clobber Mike and give solace to Aphrodite. But he remembered the last thing she had said to him before she fled his room and wondered if she ever regretted her words.

The following day, after the last school bell had rung, Heath was walking towards his locker when he found Aphrodite crouched on the floor, gathering her scattered books. Based on the distraught look on her face, he knew someone had tripped her. She finished collecting her things and stormed away, not even acknowledging him.

On Wednesday, Heath arrived at his algebra II class but was surprised to discover Aphrodite wasn't in her seat. Unable to focus, he failed yet another exam. He thought maybe she had been the smart one, and had skipped the class but when he went to lunch, she wasn't there either.

Where could she be?

Aphrodite sat against the cedar hope chest, stored in the attic of the Bailey house, hugging her knees close to her as she sobbed uncontrollably. She never imagined readjusting to her old life would be this painful. She had hoped that after a few days she wouldn't miss Heath anymore but her misery seemed to grow with each passing second. She felt as if she had found what she wanted when she didn't even know she needed it, only to have it taken away. Alone with her sorrow, she thought about Henry Bailey. She finally understood why a man would dedicate his life to build a house, keep a promise to his dead wife and request to have his ashen remains combined with hers, their bodies intertwined for all eternity. Henry Bailey had loved his wife desperately, the same way she loved Heath. Heath might have felt the same way while they had been in the future, but it seemed impossible to her that he would feel the same way now. Not when she wasn't the only option anymore and especially not when she was beginning to look like her old self. She was realistic. No matter what her face or hair looked like before, she would never be as pretty as Amber or half the girls she had seen Heath flirting with at school. She was just a slightly less messy Aphrodite and his rejection seemed inevitable. She was disappointed when he didn't stop her from storming out of his house and it surprised her when she realized that she thought he would. She was beginning to think that the time traveling had fried her brain.

She remembered what Heath had said about her heart and she understood he had been right. It wasn't dead, but she could feel it preparing itself for a long slumber and she knew that without Heath, it would remain dormant for the rest of her life. She also realized that her heart was not shutting down just because of Heath. She thought of Jane, the most amazing woman she had ever encountered but would never see again and the offspring she would never get to meet. She had finally discovered a world worth saving but would never be a part of. A new barrage of tears emerged from her eyes as she mourned for her broken heart and the family she would never have.

As much as she was used to being miserable, she was giving serious thought to transferring to a different high school if she ever wanted to reclaim some semblance of a regular life. She knew it was late in the school year and her parents would most likely balk but she could threaten them with dropping out if they didn't help her, and at this point, dropping out seemed like a better option than returning to school. Until then, she was going to look into colleges in Alaska.

Aphrodite sensed someone standing at the doorway and thought she had finally been busted. But when she looked in the direction of the open door, Heath was standing there.

"Can we stop acting now?" he asked earnestly, worn from the charade. "I was hoping to do something with you this weekend." Tears of joy chased away the stream of sorrow. Wiping her face, she nodded her head, stood up and ran to him.

"I thought you'd never ask," she said and kissed him. She felt her heart stir to life once more, as it came out of its self-imposed hibernation.

Their lips moved in synch as if they had been designed only for each other.

Heath stopped so he could gaze at her, their embrace remained intact. Her dark eyes reminded him of the black hole that had nearly swallowed the earth. But unlike then, he would gladly fall into them forever.

"I love you," he declared ardently. "Did you really think I didn't?"

It pained Aphrodite when she recalled her doubt, but life is about possibilities, even ones that hurt.

"I love you, too," she murmured, "but I was

afraid that once we got back, and you saw your friends again, you'd change your mind," she said.

"And miss out on you and Jane and Mary and Apollo and I really want to discuss his name with you," he said, chuckling with her.

"Are you sure about us? You're going to be an outcast, just like me," she said, concerned with the fallout he would experience from his friends. She was used to it but she didn't want to see him suffer.

But his smile never faltered. Every time he pictured his future, Aphrodite was in every frame. He took her hands in his.

"Aphrodite, this is the first time since before my accident that I know what I want to do with my life and I'm happy. Besides, we graduate in five months and it won't matter anymore."

"Do you know what you're going to do after graduation?" she asked curiously. She never did find out what he did for a living when they were in the future. It was like he never had a job.

"Actually, I know what I'm going to do before we graduate. Have I ever told you about plan B?"

"What's plan B?" she asked, content to be in his arms.

"It's not as good as plan A," he answered.

Okay, I'll bite, she thought to herself. "What's plan A?"

"You," he said simply.

"Aww. You're just saying that cause you hope to get lucky," she teased.

"Oh, I already know I get lucky," he said suggestively and enjoyed the taste of her lips on his once more.

Realizing that he had just evaded her question rather effectively, she asked again, "What's plan B?"

"Do you trust me?"

"With my future," she replied.

Heath and Aphrodite walked out of the Bailey house, hand in hand, both still basking in the afterglow from finally professing their love. Aphrodite enjoyed the feeling of his fingers intertwined with hers, spreading shocks of delight throughout her body.

"So, what time am I picking you up tomorrow?" he asked, as they walked towards his car.

"You're picking me up?"

"Sure. I want to make sure everyone sees us together when we get to school," he said, eager to make their relationship public.

"There's going to be a lot of confused people and Amber's head will probably explode," she joked but wishing it was true.

"It'll only be a small explosion," he laughed. Remembering their headstone from the future, Heath suddenly became solemn. "Do you think that we'll be able to avoid our accident in the future? I mean, can we beat destiny?"

Aphrodite considered his question. She had never been one to believe in fate. And if she had to give up Heath so she could live a longer life, it was never going to happen.

"How do we know we weren't meant to find out about the accident beforehand so we can prevent it? Besides, I believe that we make our own destiny. You chose to save the world, I chose to go with you and we chose to be together." Pleased with her answer she awaited Heath's response.

"I chose to make us rich," he said unexpectedly and then walked away, afraid of her reaction.

"What?" He was by his car when she caught up to him. "How did this happen?" she demanded.

"Plan B. Win the lottery."

"You won the lottery?" she asked, dumbfounded.

"We," he corrected, as he fished his car keys out of his pocket.

"We won the lottery? Oh my God. You used the pen, didn't you?"

He opened the passenger side door for her, gesturing for her to get in the car.

"Yep. But how do you know we weren't meant to win it?" he said, using her own words against her. How could she argue with her own logic? Yielding to him, she sat in her seat as Heath swung her door closed. He climbed into the driver's seat and turned the key in the ignition. The Barracuda roared to life, ready for the next destination.

"It's going to be amazing, isn't it?" he marveled, looking out the front windshield, as if he could already see what lay before them.

"Because of the money?" she asked. Heath leaned over and kissed her tenderly. He ended the kiss but kept his eyes on her.

"No," he answered dreamily.

"I can't believe I'm going to be Aphrodite Wells someday," she said with incredulity.

Hearing her name reminded him of an epiphany he had had the night before. It was something that had occurred to him as he was falling asleep and kept his mind focused on her.

"About your name," he began. "I think it's beautiful but you have to admit it can be a mouthful sometimes."

Aphrodite smiled at him, curious as to where he was going with this.

"A nickname popped into my head yesterday and I was wondering..."

As they continued the conversation, Heath put the car into drive, pulled away from the curb, and began the adventure they were meant to share.

Epilogue

The pen rested in the Scribe's clutched hand, having been rescued by him. He wasn't ready to let his creation be destroyed. Its adventure wasn't done yet. After watching Heath and Aphrodite run from the garbage bin, he retrieved his treasure from where they had dumped it. He returned his gaze to where the two figures continued to run, fading into the distance. He knew that soon, they would fade back into their time and everything would be as it should. The Scribe smiled, satisfied with himself and more importantly, with the way things had turned out. When the two teens returned to their present, they would continue to lead the lives that had been predestined for them. They just needed some guidance considering that not every journey starts in the right direction.

A warm breeze blew through his salt and pepper hair, ruffling it in the same manner he did to himself when he was frustrated, causing him to smile. If Heath and Aphrodite could see him now, they would have a plethora of questions for the school counselor, none of which he would be willing to answer. He wouldn't even know where to begin. How do you put into words who you really are? What you really are? Even then they would never truly be able to understand the complexity of it all.

There was truth to the saying, “The eyes are the window to the soul.” He should know because he was the first being to coin the phrase. That axiom had become as eternal as him. He could look someone in their eyes and see beyond them. He could see their lifeline. And whenever Heath came to see him, he could see in Heath’s eyes that he was more than just a broken athlete. The trick was getting Heath to see that as well. What surprised him most though was seeing Aphrodite not only in his past and present but in his future as well. And even though Aphrodite was not one of his assigned students, he was positive that one look into her eyes would reveal a lifetime with the last person she ever expected.

Mr. Amara lightly tossed the pen into the air, catching it easily in his right hand as he thought about what they had had to endure. He could have made it easier for them and still have gotten the same result but what would have been the fun in that. He made them heroes even though the world would never know it. He had also taken a huge risk. If they had never embraced their destiny or failed in their mission, it would have changed time forever. He hoped that Bishop would overlook the risk. Bishop wasn’t pleasant when displeased.

His work was done here but he would return to his job as a school counselor. After all, that was his job and Heath and Aphrodite weren’t the only ones who needed his guidance. Besides, he was looking forward to watching their story play out. It was just beginning even though he already knew it by heart and there was a particular event he hoped they would be able to alter.

Destiny is a funny thing, he thought to himself with a sly grin as he started to phase out of time. *With the right pen, you can rewrite the future.*

About the Author

V.B. Kennedy resides in Miami, Florida, with her husband and two kids. She is also the author of *Pleasant Journey*, a collection of five short stories about a vampire coming to terms with his past and current existence. She has also written *Intensity*, a novel about a vigilante who is aided by a detective while saving a city.

Made in the USA
Columbia, SC
28 December 2022

74410802R00124